THE BOY FROM DUCK RIVER

Limited Cloth Edition

Number **499** *of 500*

KARSTEN ALNÆS

EVEN 1814

ILLUSTRERT AV
JOHAN H. F. KIPPENBROECK

AVENTURA FORLAG

The Boy from Duck River

A Norwegian Adventure Tale

by
Karsten Alnæs

Illustrated by
Johan H. F. Kippenbroeck

Edited and Translated by
Rune A. Engebretsen

NORTH STAR PRESS OF ST. CLOUD, INC.

Cover art: *Myrhorn i Jostedal* (*The Mountain Myrhorn in Jostedal*) 1822-35, by Johannes Flintoe, Nasjonalgalleriet, Oslo, Norway. The painting is gouache on paper, 79 x 65 cm. The transparency of the painting was made by J. Lathion at the courtesy of Nils Messel.

The Boy from Duck River was first published in Norwegian as *Even 1814* by Aventura Forlag, Oslo, Norway, in 1989. This is the first translation of the book into English.

ISBN: 0-87839-101-0 Paper
ISBN: 0-87839-102-9 Cloth

Printed in the United States of America by Versa Press, East Peoria, Illinois.

Published by   North Star Press of St. Cloud, Inc.
                P.O. Box 451
                St. Cloud, Minnesota 56302

Foreword

What happened at Eidsvoll, Norway, in the spring of 1814 was an adventure, a turning point in the history of a nation. Those who were there had a clear sense of participating in an hour of destiny. For the first time since the Middle Ages, Norway became an independent country, receiving the most democratic constitution in Europe. Almost fifty percent of the male population above the age of twenty-five gained the right to vote. Like the United States, Norway received what has been called a constitution for "the small freeholders." It perdures to this very day, with modifications as required by the times. It is the oldest constitution in Europe still in force.

The background for what happened in Norway in 1814 is rooted in the dissolution of the United Monarchy of Denmark-Norway. In the Napoleonic Wars, The Danish-Norwegian king had sided with Napoleon. At war's end, the king had to pay for this choice by giving up Norway. Sweden was to receive Norway in recompense for Finland, which was placed under the Russian czar. The political manipulations on a large scale created a situation conducive to freedom and to establishing the constitution in Norway. It has been said that Norway received "freedom as a gift," but the Norwegians certainly also knew how to make the most of the situation.

The leader of the Norwegian uprising was Christian Frederik, the Danish Crown prince, who had been sent to Norway as governor in 1813. Directed against the manipulations of the great powers, the uprising he spearheaded was based on the idea of national independence. Yet the prince may well have had a long-term strategy of reuniting Norway with Denmark. The march of events, however, assumed its own dynamics.

Why did the Norwegian constitution become so democratic? There was no general discontent with the bureaucratized autocracy of the United Monarchy. But with the political situation after the Napoleonic Wars and the need to rebuild Norway from the ground up, the idea of freedom spread easily. Undoubtedly, the slant of that idea came, in no small part, from the French Revolution and the example of the United States. Christian Frederik was quickly persuaded to give up his right of inheritance. He summoned a constituent assembly in order to establish a constitutional monarchy. When that was in place, he allowed himself to be elected king on May 17, 1814.

It was not long until Swedish troops, returning from the European continent, were engaged in a brief war against Norway. The armed conflict never came to a decisive battle because the outcome was decided on a diplomatic level by the great powers. Norway was allowed to keep its constitution, but it had to accept the King of Sweden as its king. This is how the Dual Monarchy of Sweden-Norway came to be. It lasted until 1905, when Norway gained full independence and chose a Danish prince as king.

But, in Norwegian national consciousness, the great year of freedom was and is 1814. The events of that year Karsten Alnæs has portrayed from an exceptional and surprising perspective in this novel.

Francis Sejersted
Professor of History, The University of Oslo
Chair, the Nobel Peace Prize Committee

Translator's Introduction

Once a year, on May 17, Norwegians gather to celebrate a special day, *syttende mai*. Dressed in folk costumes or their Sunday best, people flock together in every town and village of Norway. Thousands of school children and their teachers march at full fanfare through the streets, lined with parents and relatives, neighbors and friends, who cheer them on. One and all cry out with cheerful voices: "Hurrah for the seventeenth of May!"

In Oslo, the capital of Norway, the king and the queen—with the princess and crown prince alongside—greet the parade from the balcony of the Royal Palace. Looking down Karl Johan Street toward the Parliament and beyond, the royal family see people by the tens of thousands. A sea of colors in red, white, and blue; ribbons and flags undulate in the gentle breeze of springtide. The children marching by the palace lift their faces toward the royal balcony and wave Norwegian flags. Their voices rise with well-wishing and triple hip-hip-hurrahs. Singing, laughter, bands playing. Hour upon hour, the parade keeps coming. Hour upon hour with smiling grace, the royalty wave back to the crowds.

What are these people celebrating? They are celebrating a birthday—the birth of their country. That birth or rebirth is the story of *The Boy from Duck River*. At heart, it is a story about how people are set free.

It is also a story about Espen, eleven years old and a cottager's son, who lives at Eidsvoll, Norway. The year is 1814. On the European continent, the Napoleonic wars are drawing to a close. In Norway, a dream is beginning to emerge: the country wants to be an independent nation with its own king and constitution. At the Eidsvoll Estate, where Espen's father cares for the horses, 112 representatives—civil servants, pastors, landowners—gather to give shape to the national dream. For Espen, it is a time of hardship. His brother, Ole, is fighting in the war, and hunger is gnawing at Espen. His father, Sven, known as "the horse king," must tend to his duties at the estate. That leaves little time for Espen, but it does bring him close to some dramatic, exciting events. One day he stands face to face with the Prince of Denmark, who has come to be proclaimed King of Norway.

Amid the making of history, Espen takes the reader into the woods and valleys of the Norwegian landscape, its sights and scents. The book brims with the lore and the ways of folk culture. The shadowlands of trolls, gnomes, and the Little People is never far from Espen, nor is the high culture in the guilded halls of the mansion at Eidsvoll. Espen compares that mansion to Soria Moria, a castle of enchantment in Norwegian folk belief. Espen lives on a small cottager's plot deep in the forest. From there to the manion or up to his favorite fishing pond, he may run into danger. He may meet a *hulder,* a wood nymph, and be spirited away into the underbelly of a mountain, never again to see the light of day.

Readers often ask if a story is true. In this novel, historical places and names, statements, and events are remarkably accurate. They are, as one would say, true to the facts. But the tale about Espen is a work of the imagination. As such it expresses its own inner truth. Story or history? In witnessing the making of history, Espen makes that history his own and lives it as *his* story.

Karsten Alnæs, the author of this novel, has written both for adults and young people. *The Boy from Duck River* is Alnæs' first publication in English. The translation adheres closely to the original Norwegian version of 1989. A few minor changes have been undertaken in the text with the English-speaking reader in mind and with the approval of the author.

The Norwegian word for "Duck River" is *Andelven*, a word that carries two meanings. On the one hand, it means Duck River. On the other hand, it means "Contra-River" or "Counter-River," a river that runs in the opposite direction of another river. Whether the framers of the Norwegian constitution had this second meaning in mind when "countering" or opposing the Swedes and the Danes shall remain undecided, but it would fit the picture. In this novel, *Andelven* has been rendered as Duck River.

I wish to thank Francis Sejersted, Distinguished Professor of History at the University of Oslo and Chair of the Nobel Peace Prize Committee, for writing the foreword; Jo Benkow, President Ret. of the Parliament of Norway, for providing the afterword; and Lynell Johnson for generously imparting his superb editorial skill, this time with regard to young adult readers.

The publication is supported by grants from NORLA and the Royal Norwegian Foreign Ministry. Thanks are extended to Kristin Brudevoll, Inger Melhus-Ræder, Kjellaug Myhre, Bjarne Grindem, Gerd Pettersen, John Bjørnebye, and Bjørn Jensen. I am indebted to Lois Lindbloom for her assistance in moving this project forward. The manuscript, typed by Sylvia Larson and Lisa Roppe, has been guided through the press by Corinne and Rita Dwyer.

Rune Engebretsen
August 1995
Concordia College on the Red River of the North

I

King or Potato

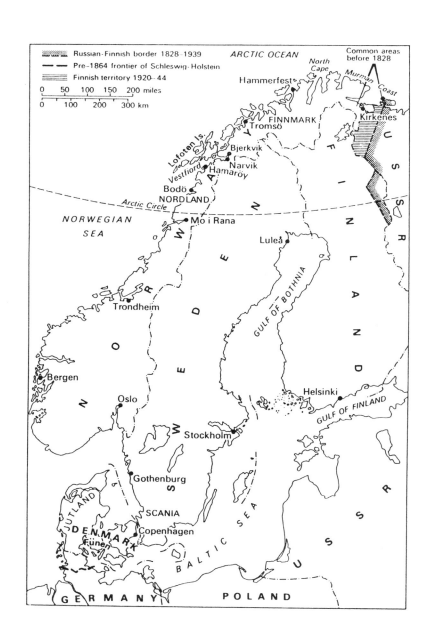

ARCTIC OCEAN

Russian-Finnish border 1828-1939	
Pre-1864 frontier of Schleswig-Holstein	
Finnish territory 1920-44	

0   50   100   150   200 miles
0   100   200   300 km

Common areas
before 1828

North
Cape

Murman
Coast

Hammerfest

FINNMARK

Kirkenes

Tromsö

Lofoten Is.

Bjerkvik

Narvik

Vestfjord Hamaröy

Bodö

NORDLAND

Arctic Circle

NORWEGIAN
SEA

Mo i Rana

Luleå

GULF OF BOTHNIA

Trondheim

Bergen

Helsinki

Oslo

GULF OF FINLAND

Stockholm

Gothenburg

SCANIA

JUTLAND

DENMARK

Copenhagen

Fünen

BALTIC SEA

GERMANY   POLAND

N O R W E D E N

F I N L A N D

U S S R

Espen woke up shivering. A hollow space grew inside him, and the darkness closed around him. He listened but heard nothing. Not a breath. He was alone. So Father had not come home from the estate last night. He had stayed and was sleeping there with his horses as usual.

Slowly Espen made out the ceiling and the walls. Light from outside came through the small, thick windowpanes and filtered through some cracks in the wall where Father had forgotten to stuff moss between the logs. Espen still felt heavy with sleep, but he raised up on his elbows, swung his legs out of bed and set his feet on the floor. The Kaarud cottage did have a wooden floor, even if the boards were rotten and a few gaps had been filled with mud.

Winter light from the window fell on the gray corner cupboard and the tabletop attached to the wall. There they had

1

eaten together when Mother was alive and Ole was at home. The soup cups were still lined up on the wooden shelf next to the window. The wooden spoons stood in their slots in the shelf like marching soldiers not willing to admit that those days were gone. But the big black wooden bowls and plates sat empty at the edge of the hearth.

From the chimney hook hung an iron pot. It still contained a swallow or two of the soup he had made the other day. He had caught a rabbit in one of his traps. The meat he had gobbled down quickly. From the bones he had made broth.

He stirred up the embers in the fireplace. A little piping-hot soup would warm him up. He needed it so that his courage would not disappear in the darkness of night. He often felt downhearted and afraid when he woke up alone like this. But daylight and warmth could lift his spirits.

Anyway, today he would be heading out to check his traps. He had set them yesterday, far up on the mountainside around Black Pond. That was where he and Ole used to set their traps. It was deep in the forest, almost in the wilderness.

No. He was not afraid. He was all of eleven years old, and the son of Sven Kaarud, "horse king" at the Eidsvoll Estate, who took care of the workhorses for none other than Carsten Anker! Yes, it was true enough that this far into the forest there were the Little People in the hills and under the rocks. Bears and wolves also roamed the rocky slopes and the woods on the heights around Black Pond. But Espen felt on good terms with the Little People. Old Anna at Buhagen had often said that he himself had *hulder* eyes—with a look of magical power—so he had no need to fear those he could not see.

Anna Buhagen also used to say that Espen was a direct descendant of the outlaws who haunted the woods in the old days. That was why there was so much wildness in him, she said. He would outlive them all, because that was what robbers did. When Anna said this, she would give his hair a good, long pull. That reminded him of Mother.

No, don't think about that. He glanced over at the spinning wheel under the corner cupboard. Then he took a ladle from a hook on the wall and stirred the rabbit soup. It was already beginning to smell good. He must have his food, or he would starve to death. That happened to folk here in the village in winter. He and Father had found Karianne Plassen in the underbrush down by Peter's Cliff very early one morning when they were on their way to the estate. She was stiff and blue around the mouth. A year before, her two little ones had died of the dysentery that had swept the countryside. Her husband had been out fighting somewhere in the war. He had been drafted as a soldier, just like Nils Buhagen and Ole.

Espen had to bring in some wood, or he would not have much of a fire. He chided himself for standing there daydreaming so early in the morning!

He went outside. The sky stretched out forest-black, with narrow river-blue streaks in the east. Blue, frosty mist rose from the creek beds, flowed around the cookhouse and the haybarn and settled like a gnome's beard around the shed.

His shoes clattered on the ice and the frozen ground of the farmyard. The sound raced into the woods standing dark and tall on the other side of the creek. Snow covered the ground, but tufts of brown grass and thistle heads stuck out, whispering that the winter was short of snow. That meant a winter of starvation, Anna Buhagen said.

But Espen would not starve to death. He would always find a bird in one of his traps, and tonight Father would probably come home from the estate. Father never stayed away for more than three days at a time. When he came, he would bring home flatbread and maybe some meat. Espen already had fresh milk from Victoria, the cow. He was the one who

3

took care of her. She was waiting for him in the barn now, but first he had to carry in some wood.

Shivering, he hurried into the house with as much wood as his arms could hold. He put a log on the fire. The flames flared up around the iron pot, big yellow flames. The soup would soon be warm.

It tasted so good. The hot broth burned his tongue and his throat. He was not full, but at least he was not so terribly hungry anymore. The frost began to loosen its grip on him. He flapped his arms and jumped up and down a bit. He lapped up some more soup and felt warm all the way up to his cheeks!

He heard a muffled, mournful "Moooo!"

"Take it easy, Victoria," he thought. "I'm coming." He ran out to the haybarn and quickly grabbed an armful of hay. Then he went into the cowbarn.

It was just like stepping inside the *hulder* mountain, quiet and warm. Bright little streams of water trickled through the cracks in the log wall. Victoria poured forth warmth. She stood there big and safe and looked him full in the face.

She knew everything about him and hid it inside her eyes. There she also kept other secrets. She looked forward into time. She knew about the Little People. But she said nothing.

"Now, now, my cow." Espen chatted with her while feeding her the hay. He pressed his cheek against her nose, stroked her back. He told her about Father's not coming home, about the angry cold, about the frosty mist that thickened about the walls. He brought her several buckets of water from the well. He milked her and lapped up the fresh milk.

He had better be heading for the woods now. He checked to see if hook and line were in the knapsack, then dug for worms in the manure pile under the cowbarn. There they were: big, fat earthworms. As long as there was manure, there was bait. Fish meant extra food through the long winter.

His skis were in the shed. He put them on, buttoned his jacket, pulled his cap down over his ears, and glided across the ditch and down toward the woods.

Of all the farms in the area, Kaarud was farthest into the forest. The ground had been cleared ages ago. Here peasants had acquired their own land, but Espen's grandfather had sold the place to the estate. He had gone deep into debt, people said, and he had to sell his land so that the sheriff would not send him to prison. Before that time, the folks at Kaarud had been their own lords. They hunted and fished as they pleased. They made tar. They transported iron, lumber, and even people who were willing to pay for the ride.

Ole used to say that the folks at Kaarud had been outlaws. But that was an outright lie, said Father. Ole was a liar, like the grandfather who had lied away the farm. Or was it perhaps the liquor that had tricked him? Liquor and lies amounted to about the same thing, said Father. They were God's severe punishment on people.

But even if it was a lie, Espen liked to think that those who had lived there before him had been outlaws. Wild and unruly, driven out and away. They had to have that kind of wildness in body and spirit in order to make it in such rough country. His cheeks warmed when he thought of it.

Even so, the cold air stung his face. He wondered if he should not make a quick stop at Buhagens before heading into the woods. They were the closest neighbors.

A small cluster of houses huddled together on the crest of a ridge. The fields stretched bigger and wider here than at Kaarud.

"My, my, if it isn't Espen himself," said Old Anna when he entered the cottage. She hunched up in the bunkbed over by the window and squinted to see better. Would he like a piece of flatbread?

"No, thanks. I just ate," he said, "I'm just on my way to

5

the woods to check my traps." He wondered where the rest of the Buhagens might be.

"Remember to watch out for the wolves," said Old Anna. "And the goblins and the robbers. You know there are all kinds of creatures roaming aboveground and underground."

Well, he didn't mind either ghosts or monsters. But wasn't anyone home besides her?

Nils was in the war, fighting as a soldier just like Ole. Anna moaned and groaned when she talked about the war. It was nothing but misery, she said.

And Ingrid, the mistress of the house and her daughter-in-law, was down at the estate doing baking chores. As for Old Anna's son Jens and little Kristine, well, if she could only remember where they were!

"Here we are," sounded a voice behind Espen. There stood Jens with an armful of firewood, chuckling. Little Kristine, waddling behind her father, gave Espen a big smile.

"Are you going to check your traps?" she asked. Espen had once promised Kristine that she could go with him into the forest, but that would have to wait until summer. Today it was biting cold, and he was going much too far into the forest to drag along a little bundle like her.

"I just dropped by to say a quick hello. I don't want to keep anybody," said Espen.

"That's a good thing," said Jens and chuckled again. "We're terribly busy at Buhagen these days."

He gave Espen a sidelong look. Espen realized that Jens had been teasing him. But seeing the man's eyes, so calm and kind, Espen understood that his neighbor wished him well. So he stayed a little longer and chatted with the folks at Buhagen. Finally he had to be on his way. He had hoped that Jens might also be heading for the woods today, but he did not seem to have time.

* * *

Once again the cold grabbed hold of him. The sky rose white and naked. His skis crackled and crunched dryly between the tree trunks. He heard nothing except this sound, nor did he notice anything. An hour passed. What if he met a wolf? Or ran into an evildoer? He had heard about such people, runaways from the army or murderers on the hunt for young girls and boys.

He followed a ravine up to a lake high in the woods. It was rough going, but he struggled up, feeling hunger begin to rumble and gnaw through his body. At the same time, anxiety gripped him.

He was no longer sure he would live until the next spring. He was no longer sure that Father would come home that night. Maybe he would never come home again! Maybe Espen would die up on the slopes or someplace in the forest. Many cottagers' children had starved to death in the last few years of the war. He was worse off than most, especially now after Mother's death.

Those lies were turning up and making him lose his wits! Lies and liquor, Father had said. They were humankind's worst enemies. But wasn't he an outlaw, a he-man who knew the forest better than anybody else? Of course he was. He would make it!

He shouldn't be thinking about trolls or wolves or his mother or that brother of his, who was lying in the trenches somewhere, fighting the Swedes.

Espen quickened his pace, but he felt weak.

The forest turned into a thicket of juniper bushes, alders, goat willows, birches. The little ski trail he had been following disappeared among the boulders. The tracks of a fox ran to and fro in a clump of trees.

Here inside the thicket he had set the first trap! No, nothing there. The bait was still in place. He covered over his footprints and hurried to the next place. Panting and puffing, blowing clouds in the air, he soon ran out of breath. His throat felt hot and dry. The next trap was set between two rocks, inside a thicket, right above the icebound, slippery-slick brook, among stiff, yellow stalks that crunched under his skis. The heat rose to his cheeks.

"Now what . . ." he said aloud. He stood there and gasped. The noose was empty. No bird in the trap. Somebody had been here! The reeds round about had been trampled. Drops of blood had trickled onto the ground, and they were round and shiny, not frozen, not dried. Someone had removed the prey, stolen the catch, run off with it. And the thief had just been here! He could not be far away. Perhaps he was hiding behind a rocky outcrop in the thicket! Who could it be? A cottager?

Or was it the fox whose tracks he had just seen? Or the *hulder* people? Maybe the goblins were making fun of him. Maybe they planned to seize him and bring him together with a *hulder* girl! Then he would be doomed to remain underground in darkness!

No. He mustn't stand there and work himself into a fit. He had to get himself to the next trap. It was on the other side of Black Pond, over the ridge, inside the gorge, where Black Pond Creek had carved out a crack and tumbled down the slope on the other side. Espen quickly slipped in between the boulders. He stopped to listen for wood grouse. Then he sped on. But, out of breath, he had to slow down little by little.

It must have been an animal that had stolen his catch, a fox or a bird of prey.

He had to put it out of his mind. It was no use thinking about it now. His forehead was wet, and he felt warm all the way down to the soles of his feet. At least he was not freezing to death right now!

But suddenly it rushed through him like a flash of lightning. He knew it before he could get hold of himself, and the fright nearly struck him to the ground: Somebody was following him! He didn't know where the thought came from. He swiftly turned on his heel.

Down in the thicket, among the dense snow-covered junipers and in the alder brushwood, a sun-lighted mist crawled in a slow rolling motion. The black twigs shone brightly wet.

There was no sign of life. But he could feel a presence in his bones. Down in the wood brush, behind a rock, someone was watching him!

Before he could complete his thought, he heard a voice that scared him stiff and made him numb from head to toe:

"Hey, fellow!"

Espen did an about-face. And there, up on a boulder, stood an outlaw, a man with a gun, a fellow in gray, tattered clothing! He could barely make out the figure because the rays of the sun shot straight into his eyes. He shaded them, but it didn't help much.

"Hey, Espen, did you catch the forest-fright?"

The robber knew him. He called him by name! Espen had heard stories about outlaws in the woods, criminals who escaped the gallows, murderers, and heathens.

"I scared you out of your wits, didn't I? Are you afraid, boy?"

There was something familiar about the voice. And the robber talked as if he meant no harm.

"It's me—Ole. Don't you recognize me?"

Ole? His brother? His brother the soldier! But then a soldier did not look like that. His pants had a wide-open rip in the crotch. The arm of his jacket hung in tatters. On his feet the soldier wore rags instead of newly polished boots. His face was drawn, just skin and bones, and ash-gray, as if he were sick.

While Espen stared, just beginning to believe it was Ole, the man had caught up with him. He threw his arms around

Espen, swung him around, shouted for joy, rolled him on the ground, ran after him, wrestled him to the ground again, and lifted him up.

"I scared the daylights out of you, didn't I? But look!" He held up a wood grouse. "You are a terrific trapper, you know!"

Then they were off to Black Pond.

At Black Pond, right beneath a crag, they gathered kindling and dry wood, built a fire and made a bed of evergreens on the ground. Ole plucked the bird and took out some odd-looking apples he had in his satchel.

"Look," he said. "Do you know what these are?"

"Apples," said Espen. He was not so stupid that he did not know what an apple was.

"You are either a blockhead or a Turk," said his brother good-naturedly. "This is not an apple, not by a long shot."

Espen did not know what a Turk was. Maybe one of those awful people Ole had fought in the war. The last time Ole had come home he had said that he was at war with the English, the Germans, the Swedes, and the Gypsies, and since that time he had perhaps started to fight the Turks, too.

His brother was always full of strange words. Espen could never figure him out.

Ole held the small reddish thing in his hand. "This is a potato, and you are supposed to eat it. It comes from a pastor down in Arendal, and it tastes good. In America, people eat potatoes all day long, and in Africa potatoes grow on trees."

That brother of his knew a lot! The flames from the fire warmed their hands and faces. The brothers added a little kindling and threw on some windfallen birch branches. Ole whittled some wooden spits and skewered the potatoes on them.

"There will be war with the Swedes again," Ole said.

Espen did not care much for war. There had been war against the Swedes as long as he could remember. But that was going on some other place, someplace far away. It might as well have been a fairy tale. Sometimes it was better not to think of such things. Espen looked into the flames and smelled the tempting aroma of wood grouse. Ole had better not burn it now.

"But, you see, there'll be war now!" said Ole excitedly. "The Swedes have gotten a crown prince who doesn't want anything but war."

"Yes, sir," answered Espen.

"His name is Carl Johan, and he is French and all that. All he wants is to conquer Norway—all the farms, the forests, the cities, and all the silver in Kongsberg—because if he can't do it, the Swedes don't want him as king. He is a Frenchman, you know."

Espen could certainly understand that it would not be easy to have a Frenchman for a crown prince.

"You see, the Swedes lost to the Russians. That's why they chose a French warrior to fight for them. If he makes a go of it, they'll have him as king. If things go badly, they'll send him back to the manure pile."

Espen inched closer to the warmth of the fire.

"But I'll tell you something," said Ole. "It won't be easy for him. There is also someone else who wants to be king here in our country. Guess who."

Espen had no idea, nor did he much care. Frederik in Copenhagen was king of Denmark and Norway. That he knew. He also knew that Frederik and the great French war chief Napoleon were on the same side in the war. They fought the Russians, the Prussians, the Austrians, and also the English. He had heard people say this. And his father talked about it quite a bit, because out there in the world, in the cities and on the battlegrounds, great and important things were happening. But the English, who were enemies of Frederik in Copenhagen, had sailed their battleships to Norway and were lying in wait off the coast. They blockaded all the harbors and sank the ships with gunfire, or they rushed aboard with drawn swords, stole the cargo, and locked the crew below decks.

It was the English who blockaded the country. They were the ones who kept the grain ships from reaching Norway with barley and rye from Denmark and Germany. They were the ones to blame for making little Lina starve to death last spring down on the Nordli farm.

"Before the English came with their gunboats, nobody in our village went hungry," Father had said. That had been such a long time ago that Espen could not remember it—but he believed it. Maybe the English were also the ones who wanted their king to rule Norway.

"Guess who wants to become king," Ole repeated.

Espen did not know.

"The Danish crown prince, Christian Frederik, the one who came as a naval recruit to our country. He himself wants to become King of Norway."

Espen did not understand. Then the country would have two Danish kings, Frederik in Copenhagen and Christian Frederik, who had been sent to Norway by Frederik to fight against the Swedes and the English.

"No, no, then Norway will have its own king. There will be one king in Denmark and one in Norway," said Ole. "It will be as it was long ago when powerful kings ruled the country: St. Olaf, Olaf Trygvasson, Harald the Fairhaired. You have heard about them, haven't you?"

No, Espen had never heard about them, and now he was worried that the grouse would be burned.

"Everybody says that Christian Frederik will be king of our country. He will make Norway an independent kingdom!"

As far as Espen was concerned, Christian Frederik could do as he pleased. Ole was back home now. His big brother was sitting there dirty and tattered, handing him a round fruit that had been baked in the fire!

13

And did that potato ever taste good! Ole had sprinkled on some salt that he had brought along. The fruit was soft and juicy and tasted of America and Africa. Ole explained that it grew in Norway, too. Quite a few pastors raised it.

There were so many strange things in this world. When he grew up, Espen would travel and see all those wondrous things.

He wanted to go to sea. He wanted to pick potatoes from the trees in Africa and roam about in the big cities that were supposed to be out there in the world. That is where things were happening. Here at home, everything was so stuffy and quiet. People spoke to one another in low voices and dragged themselves slowly along the roadsides, burdened with worries about tomorrow. Out there in the world, people fired huge cannons and ate bacon and beans every day.

"I think we had better have a taste of that bird now," said Ole. He removed the grouse from the embers and began to carve it with his big soldier's knife.

"This is even better than lamb and honey."

There they sat, each with a juicy chunk of fowl between his teeth, and felt like kings. The flames made them hot. Little by little, as their stomachs filled up, they grew cheerful. Then they dozed off because they were not used to having their fill.

They roused a little while later to put more wood on the fire. "Come here and I'll show you my gun," said Ole, hefting the big weapon. "Here is the flintlock, here the flint jams in place, and here I put the primer. There aren't very many who have a gun like mine. I took it over after Jens," he said seriously. "He died of dysentery last year. And this ramrod I have from Hans, who deserted before Christmas. And here I have forty-six cartridges," he said proudly. "That's more than anybody else in our company. And now King Frederik in Copenhagen says that each one of us is supposed to have sixty cartridges, but we are running short of guns, cartridges, uniforms, boots, and food. Let me tell you, Espen, the Norwegian army is a gang of hoboes."

Espen looked at his brother: At the cheekbones that stuck out from his thin, drawn face. At the rags around his legs. At the rips in his jacket and his pants. At the shabby knapsack he carried on his back.

"But we do know how to fight!" Ole suddenly exclaimed. He jumped to his feet, snapped the bayonet onto the gun barrel, and jabbed it into an invisible enemy. "Take a Swede with you into the next life," he hollered. "Death or freedom!"

Then he sat down. "Father hasn't found a sweetheart since I left, has he?" He looked at his brother.

In silence, Espen shifted his weight from foot to foot. "I really don't think there are any cottagers' girls left for Father,"

15

Espen finally responded. "He has gotten too old for them, and Kaarud is so far off the beaten path—and not exactly Soria Moria Castle! You know, Father has become a stableman of sorts for Carsten Anker at the estate. More than that! He has become a confidant."

"Confidant?" Ole said.

Espen noticed that Ole did not understand the word. That was too bad, because he didn't understand it either. Father had used it one evening when he came home.

"I suppose Father has taken to the bottle for comfort," Ole said, as if asking a question. He gazed into the root of a toppled spruce tree. He did not look in Espen's direction.

Espen did not respond.

"He probably has," Ole confirmed. "He probably longs for a young wife. But then he is in charge of the stables at Carsten Anker's estate," Ole said slowly, as if talking to himself. "And Carsten Anker realizes that Sven Kaarud is smarter than most."

Espen listened.

"And Carsten Anker is Prince Christian Frederik's best friend. The two of them often discuss how Christian Frederik will become king of Norway. And Carsten Anker talks with his stableman, and then Father forgets that he is a cottager and lives in the deep woods and has a little lad who spends a lot of time alone."

Ole gazed into the fire. "I am nothing but a wretched soldier, Espen. I have no oats in my satchel, no boots on my feet, and no sense in my head. I am out fighting a war for clergymen, judges, bishops, county officials, and estate owners such as Carsten Anker, the prince's best friend, who walks around in silk and knee-pants all day long and eats white bread until his stomach bursts."

"But," said Espen, "you have said yourself that Christian Frederik will become king of Norway and turn Norway into an independent kingdom."

"Let me tell you something," said Ole with a laugh, grabbing his gun and skipping like a weasel behind a rock. Bouncing and climbing to the top, he shouted out over Black Pond: "This is Napoleon! Napoleon is coming to Black Pond. The French emperor is ordering all Hedmarkers, Opplanders, and Valdresians to go to hell. The French emperor commands Carsten Anker to be hanged, Prince Christian Frederik of Denmark-Norway to dress like a woman, and Espen Kaarud to eat potatoes every day."

"Gladly," chuckled Espen.

"But don't you understand?" said Ole on top of the rock. "Don't you understand that Napoleon is the one who makes the difference? If Emperor Napoleon wins the war against England and Russia, then Denmark and King Frederik will also be victors. But if England and Russia beat the boots off the French, Frederik will also be defeated. And then Carsten Anker and Prince Christian Frederik and Sven Kaarud can all go and jump in the lake."

Espen looked southward. Far away, on the big plains in those big countries, thousands upon thousands of soldiers were marching forth in red and blue uniforms, with swords, cannons, and guns, with drums and trumpets. He wanted Napoleon to win, even though his father had told him that the troops belonging to the French emperor had had the life frozen out of them in the icy heart of Russia. There were not many French soldiers left. But those who survived fought so hard the dirt flew.

Nobody could fight like the French, except perhaps Norwegians such as Ole, Per, and Nils—cottagers' sons from his home community whom he knew to be the gutsiest anywhere. Someday he wanted to be like them, to be a fighting hero, or maybe something even greater than they were, like Sigurd the Dragon-Slayer or Strong Knut, who killed three bears with his bare hands and brought the princess out of the

17

snake pit. Espen had heard the story about Askeladden, who entered an eating contest with a troll. Jens Oppistuen had told him about giants and warriors, about knights and men who were strong like no one else. Against them, even Em-peror Napoleon became a pushover.

"But now we'd better catch some fish and then find our way home," said Ole.

Once again they cut open the hole in the ice at Black Pond, took out some bait and line and lit a fire on the ice. They flapped their arms to stay warm, and it helped. But the fish would not bite. They pulled up a few small fry. Ole thought that was barely enough for the cat. Then they skied home, carved the rest of the wood grouse, built a fire and fed Victoria.

Later in the evening, the door handle turned. It was Father. "My, my, are you here, Ole?" he said. But he did not look particularly happy about his son being home. In the last year, Father had become thin and pale. His eyes kept flitting about the room, looking for something on which to focus. He could not find his voice, and, searching for words, he sat down on a stool and looked at his feet. "There is big news out there in the world," said Father.

"I doubt it," answered Ole. "No matter how big the news is, it doesn't do us any good when we are starving to death."

"Peace has been declared," said Father. "The war is over."

Ole stared at Father in amazement, his mouth open.

"And something else has happened, too. Denmark has surrendered in the battle against Sweden and England. The Danish king has been forced to his knees. He is defeated, he is finished, and he has given up Norway."

"Are we under the Russians now?" Ole asked.

"No, Norway has been given to Sweden. Given away like a piece of cake."

"It isn't much of a piece," Ole said. "It's mostly poverty and lice."

"Carsten Anker received a message from Kiel yesterday," said Father. "There is no doubt about it. The old Kingdom of Norway that has lived in peaceful union and marriage with Denmark for four hundred years has been given to the Swedish king, Charles XV. And the crown prince, Carl Johan, has every reason to be thrilled. It is his plan."

"I don't mind becoming a Swede if I can have oatmeal and pickled herring," said Ole. "And Victoria will gladly become a Swede cow as long as she can eat green grass in the summer."

"Carsten Anker says that we mustn't give up," continued Father. "The fight isn't over yet. People say that he'll make

Christian Frederik the King of Norway and that the free Norway of old will rise again."

"Norway here and Norway there; you can take Norway and wipe my rear," answered Ole. "I have trudged around in this raggedy country all winter. People don't need kings and Napoleons. They need herring, grain, meat, and clothing. They need God's peace and blessing."

"You don't understand much," said Sven Kaarud. "Not that I understand so much either. But something is about to happen in our country, something that people will talk about for a thousand years."

"Let me tell you one thing," answered Ole. "I think that a bigshot like Carsten Anker should improve the living conditions for all the poor people who are burning up their lungs making glass for him, those who are slaving on their cottager's plots, and those who are living like animals in the forest cutting his lumber for him. It doesn't do us any good if he installs a prince as king. I don't need a king, I need food."

He held up a potato to his father's face.

"This is more important than a Norwegian king. This is a gold nugget that can keep people alive."

II

The Prince at Eidsvoll

B ut Sven Kaarud was glowing with excitement over what had happened. The horse king, as he was called, had lived for so long under the rich landowner Carsten Anker, that he had caught the same fire in his heart.

King Frederik had been forced to give up Norway. Norway had been handed over to Sweden.

"But Norway isn't yet tied to Sweden," Father said to Espen and Ole. They were sitting by the hearth in front of the open fire, eating the rest of the meat from the wood grouse. It was evening, with frost outside. The walls were crackling. Espen could hardly believe that both his father and brother were sitting there together with him. He was no longer alone. Tonight they would be sleeping in their cottage together, and tomorrow he would accompany Father to the estate.

"But what about Victoria?" he asked.

"Oh, you'll probably have to trudge back here in the evening and take care of the cow," answered Father.

"I'll be here for a few days," said Ole. "Espen can stay with you until the day after tomorrow. You know, I'm such a wandering bird that I like being at Kaarud."

How fortunate to have such a brother. Espen would not have minded a bit staying home and roaming the woods with his brother. But he sensed that Father needed him. Father often said that he was getting old. Soon the boys would leave home for the big world out there, and then he would be left behind in these desolate woods—that is, if he could hold on to the place. Carsten Anker might not own the land around here forever. With the war and hard times, nobody really knew what was coming. Many said that, sure as can be, the world was heading for Judgment Day. Everyone's sins would soon be announced on the church green by one of Our Lord's angels, and punishment would follow.

"Father has been listening too much to the preachers who make the rounds from farm to farm and talk about sins and Judgment Day," whispered Ole to Espen while Father was outside on a little errand. "They are swarming all over the countryside these days. You'll find them in every barn, bleating away, and people go crazy and think they'll boil in the cauldrons of hell. But I think there's enough with the hell we already have in this life," sighed Ole, and for the first time Espen realized that his brother had his bad days.

The next morning, Espen and Father skied the six miles to the Eidsvoll Estate. Espen was struck with wonder whenever he entered the courtyard of the estate and stood before the main building, which looked like a white wooden queen. He had always imagined that a fairytale castle would look like that: wing upon wing, window after window of shiny glass, big doors with polished handles and ornamented fittings. An English master carpenter had magically created the Eidsvoll Estate

24

from the old rickety houses that had been standing there before. That master carpenter could ride on the North Wind, people said. Now he was back with the prince of England and would soon journey to Soria Moria Castle and repair the gold braids that held the castle up in the air.

Entering the stables, Espen and his father were met with the smell of horses and the warmth coming off the low ceilings. Father began to hustle and bustle right away. Farmhands ran in and out. Something was going on. Soon a servant girl came dashing across the stable floor looking for Sven, to bring him to the estate owner. Sven was over at the smithy with a horse, and the girl ran there.

In the meantime, Espen had started to feel heavy and limp, dizzy with the heat and activity of the place. He had to get out. He put on his skis and cut across the fields, across the ice of Duck River, down toward the glassworkers' huts in the north grove. But the faintness did not leave him. Was he getting sick?

He began to freeze, and stomped back to the main building. Passing close by the southern wing, he heard a sound like that of glass being crushed. The sound continued. It rose and fell. Although he knew it was against the rules, he pressed his face against the windowpane and peered inside. He saw a woman seated by a small cabinet. From the cabinet came a wondrous melody. He had heard Father say that in the homes of the wealthy, people played such music boxes. This one sounded gentler than a fiddle. The tones were sore and sad, as if they were weeping.

Then he suddenly understood that this was the mistress of the estate. She was mourning her young daughter who had died. She could never forget her. So this is how it was, even in royal mansions. There the queen and the king mourned when one of the princesses was carried away by the North Wind or spirited away into the mountains by a troll. The mistress at

26

Eidsvoll could not forget, could not stop thinking of her daughter Beate. Espen had heard people talk about it. Now he had heard it and seen it himself. Inside that window, hidden behind flowing fabric and wrapped in a light that reminded him of the catchfly flower, sat a woman playing melodies that cut him to the quick.

He was still dizzy and still felt tired, sleepy, heavy. He made his way to the cowbarn. Up in the hayloft, at the farther end, he found his spot where he slept whenever he stayed with his father. The servant girls and the farmhands also slept there, and sometimes Father would show up and sleep there—that is, when he was not staying overnight in the stables.

The hay was warm. He had never figured out how it could be warmer there than at home in front of the fireplace. But at night, the fellows and the girls, the children and the grown-ups huddled together, and sometimes even a dog would come along and nestle among them. Then they would twine themselves together into one big Noah's ark.

At the moment, he lay there alone. It was unheard-of to crawl into the bin in the middle of the afternoon. But he simply could not take it anymore. Soon he was sound asleep, with wild ducks flying through his head. They were transformed princesses on their way to the outermost skerries, the far reaches, farther than any ship could sail, even beyond the reach of Napoleon himself. But one day he, Espen Kaarud, would get there astride a big eagle. He would throw his silver cloak over the youngest of the ducks, and the bird would open its arms. See, it was Beate, the Princess of Eidsvoll! And when she opened her mouth to speak, no words came out, only strange and sorrowful sounds as if someone were crushing precious glass.

* * *

Espen woke with a jolt. Where was he? Was it day, morning, night? People were shouting. People were running. The dry snow was creaking. Was he hearing the trampling of horses?

Espen swept the hay aside. He felt an arm resting on his hip, the arm of a young farm maiden, the round, soft curve of her underarm.

Outside in the courtyard, people were moving about. And inside, in the hayloft, people were sleeping. What was that supposed to mean? Had they overslept? It was pitch dark.

Espen tumbled to his feet, climbed down from the hayloft, and stumbled out of the barn into the courtyard.

What he saw there was unbelievable.

Two large sleighs waited in the courtyard. His father held the reins of one of the four horses hitched up to the first sleigh. It was a broad-sleigh, with two double seats facing each other. Two lanterns shown on raised bayonets glittering in the night. A man in a big bearskin coat had risen to his feet. In the back of the sleigh, more bayonets and uniforms glittered in the darkness.

Not until then did Espen feel how the cold stung him. The crisp, clear sky sparkled with stars; the house walls creaked and groaned; the white horses puffed and steamed. Carsten Anker, standing toward the front of the first sleigh, greeted the company most respectfully. The soldiers and the distinguished gentleman in the bearskin coat jumped out and talked together as they picked their way toward the mansion. Many of the servants were up and hard at work. One stood by the entrance with a trayful of mugs.

What was going on? Had something happened? Who were the soldiers? Who was the gentleman in the bearskin coat?

The door remained ajar, and Espen followed the people as if in a dream. He paused outside, looking in. The soldiers

28

stood in the hallway. Some had more shiny buttons and sewed-on ribbons than others. The most distinguished one— he had to be a general—lifted his tin mug and said, "To His Majesty, King Frederik VI, in honor of his birthday."

The man in the bearskin coat locked arms with Carsten Anker, and the two of them disappeared behind a door. The soldiers remained in the hallway. The one with all the buttons said in a loud voice:

"To our beloved vice-regent, Christian Fredrik, whom we pledge to protect with our blood, him who by right of inheritance will defend our independence!"

Had Espen come to the king's court? Was he part of a fairy tale?

"Long live Prince Christian!" one of the soldiers cried out. Another caught a glimpse of Espen peeking in the door.

"Here is a Swedish spy," he shouted with a laugh, and grabbed the lad. "Let's hang the Swedish spy! Death to Carl Johan and his bootlickers!"

The man in the bearskin coat suddenly opened the door and reentered the hallway.

"Long live Prince Christian!" shouted the soldier.

"I thought I heard you gentlemen shouting something about a Swedish spy."

"Here he is," laughed the soldier who had grabbed hold of Espen. "Here is the most dangerous warrior among the Swedes."

"And what is your name, my lad?" asked the bearskin coat.

"My name is Espen Svensen Kaarud, eleven years old and a trapper," answered Espen. "And who are you?"

The bearskin coat chuckled, but Carsten Anker, who had also stepped out, looked startled.

"My name is Christian Frederik, and right now I do not know what I am," said the bearskin coat. "But I do know that no Norwegian is going to turn Swede!"

"Hurrah!" shouted the soldiers.

"And I am no Swede," said Espen. But he also remembered very well what his brother Ole had said: I'll gladly turn Swede if I can have enough oatmeal and pickled herring.

But Espen did not dare say that. Instead he added: "I've heard that it won't be easy to fight Carl Johan."

At that remark, Prince Christian turned quite serious. Then he said, "Three hundred Akershusian sharpshooters are now pulling into Akershus Fortress."

"Hurrah!" shouted the soldiers.

"Six hundred sharpshooters are on the move toward Kongsvinger. The skiers of Østerdal are rushing to the barricades at Elverum."

"Hurrah!"

Espen realized that because Christian wanted to fight, now Ole had to head out again and shoot his gun and jab his bayonet. Then Father had been right about one thing: Christian Frederik, who until now had been prince, aimed at becoming king.

"He has the right of inheritance to Norway," said a soldier, after Christian Frederik and Carsten Anker had once again disappeared behind the door.

Espen knew what right of inheritance was. He had the right of inheritance to Victoria if his father died. That is, he and Ole had the right of inheritance to the cow. And that is how it was with Christian Frederik. He would inherit Norway, just as little Kristine Buhagen, down the hill from Kaarud, had told him that she would inherit the goat when Old Anna died.

"No, he doesn't have the right of inheritance," said the man with all the shiny buttons. "The Norwegian people have the right of inheritance. That's what I have read in a number of books."

Things got quiet.

"The Norwegian people?" asked one of the soldiers in disbelief. "Precisely," said Mr. Shiny Button. "You and I, the local judge and the farmer, the merchant and the pastor, we are the ones who will inherit the country of Norway when the king of Denmark can no longer rule over it."

"But we must have a king, don't you think?"

This time another soldier asked the question, and Espen was glad he did, because Mr. Shiny Button was completely out of his mind. Of course a country must have a king. Wasn't there always a king at the head of the stairs, waiting for people when they arrived at court?

"Yes, we must have a king," said Mr. Shiny Button. "But he must be watched by the people so that he will govern with justice. A national assembly has to make laws and keep him in line so he won't go wage war and commit crimes and carry on with all kinds of trickery."

31

They had never heard anything like it, nor had Espen. He knew many fairy tales about kings, but he had never heard about this strange thing called a national assembly. What was that?

"The captain must have turned stark, raving mad," said one of the soldiers when Mr. Shiny Button had vanished from sight. "What is a national assembly?"

Nobody knew.

"They are supposed to have something like it down in France, at least they did before Napoleon seized power," said somebody else. "It had bigshots in it, chosen by the people to run the country for them."

"How many were in it?" somebody asked.

"Probably a few hundred of them," answered the smart soldier.

"We want the prince as king," said another soldier, "not a Swede, not a Spaniard, not a national assembly. Things will be in an awful mess if the bigshots end up governing the country together with the king. I would rather have a loaf of rye bread than a national assembly."

"Hurrah!" shouted the other soldiers.

Espen stepped outside into the courtyard. The stars on high were brimming with light. The village snuggled small and pitiful at the edge of the forest. Troll smoke rose white from the creek beds and from Duck River. A dog barked from one of the cottager's fields. Whenever a winter night sparkled like this, he felt so merry and joyful. It occurred to him that the world stretched out beside a long, precious road and that he could simply wander off.

The day before, he had been alone deep in the forest, hungry and scared. Today he had talked with a prince who was going to be king, and both father and Ole were nearby. He did not dare to think the thought through. Maybe the war would soon be over. Maybe Ole would come back from another stint of soldiering, and his father would find himself a new wife, and the prince would become King of Norway. And imagine that he knew all three of them!

The warmth wafted toward him as he entered the cow-barn. Some of the farm maids tottered past him in the dark on their way to early chores. He himself crawled into his lair, found himself a back to lie against, doubled up and fell asleep.

* * *

The next morning he found Father in the stables and asked him right away if he knew what a national assembly was.

"A national assembly?" No, Father did not know.

Espen went over to one of the other stablemen, who was busy sweeping away manure.

"A national assembly?" The farmhand spat on the floor. "Sounds like the devil's work."

"National assembly?" said Jens Pigtender over in the pigpen. "That must be the king's wife."

Espen gave up. He had better get back home to Kaarud. He missed his brother. Here at Eidsvoll, there was so much commotion around Prince Christian that it made his head spin. Later in the day, when Espen came across Father in the courtyard, Father thought it would be just fine for him to head home.

Father was busy hitching up horses to a sleigh, waiting for Carsten Anker, who just then came out of the mansion with a servant by his side. He was dressed in yellow knee-pants and a blue jacket, with a scarf fluttering in the wind.

"There will be no trip for us today, Sven," he said with trembling voice. "You see, I'll be going on a longer journey."

The servant looked a bit embarrassed. Carsten Anker was a man of rank who should not be talking with a stableman like Sven Kaarud. It was strange that he did so. Espen had also heard other servants express shock over the estate owner's forming a friendship with Sven. Why should Carsten Anker, whose brother was governor of Trankebar and who owned land and forest everywhere and was the prince's best friend— now why should he talk with Sven Kaarud? Why didn't he send a farmhand to do it for him?

"Everything is changing now," said Carsten Anker. "We must prepare the house for a large meeting. I myself may soon journey to England in order to keep Norway from falling into the hands of Carl Johan. We cannot allow our country to be shackled into slavery, Sven Kaarud. We would rather die."

Carsten Anker turned on his heel and went inside. Espen and his father cast a long glance in his direction.

"Well," said Father, "I think you'd better head home to Kaarud, Espen."

But for some reason or other, Espen did not leave until late in the evening, after it had turned dark, and an icy cold wind had begun to sweep across forest and field. He put on his skis, leaned forward, and thrust himself into the strong head-wind across the farmland. He felt ill at ease, for the wind whistled terribly in the brushwood. The sky was low, the stars were gone, and the evening came down nearly pitch dark upon him.

He had a long way to go. Kaarud was located far up the mountainside, higher than any other cottager's place and deeper into the forest.

He stuck to the fields and stretches of meadows as long as he could. But he had a sneaking suspicion that somebody was following him. Didn't he hear skis crackling against the crusty snow? Now and then he thought he heard a groan as if from a sick man. Was someone lying in the creek bed, moaning with pain?

It occurred to him that he ought to drop by Buhagens' place to say hello to Kristine and have a talk with Jens. He felt something pulling him in that direction. But another force told him that he ought to head home to Kaarud, the sooner the better. Somebody was waiting for him at home. He should not be dawdling along the way. So he steered a straight course.

Suddenly a huge shadow flapped across the road right in front of him. He could not see what it was, but it was not anything human.

"Listen, boy, it's probably a moose," he said aloud to put himself at ease. His voice faded away among the trees, and he was left standing there, even more alone than before. Alongside a big fallen spruce, he heard shrill sounds as if some-one were sharpening knives and at the same time gasping with laughter.

Suddenly he was struck with fear. His chest felt hollow and empty. He felt sick to his stomach, his throat dried up and ached, the horror choked him and threatened to suffocate him. He could barely move his skis.

He heard the grating sounds again, grinding, stabbing sounds: *ish-ee, ish-ee, gwee.* Was it a hand with claws, rasp-ing in the darkness up ahead? Was it the mad ogres who want-ed to whisk him away? Or could it be the tramps who wanted him for food? He had not behaved the way he should have lately. He had had nasty thoughts about Father, and he had picked up a lot of swearing from Jens Buhagen, who was def-initely no angel of God. Jens did not even bother to make the sign of the cross upon his cattle and his house, as Father always did.

Now the robbers in the forest were coming to get him, or was it a pack of trolls, or perhaps the devil himself? Espen had heard that the devil would often go after evildoers point-blank.

He gazed into the darkness. He heard the sounds again. Somebody was cackling by himself. Could it be Old Scratch, or was it a forest troll, or—then he knew. It was a ghost lying in wait for him, a spirit who that very evening had risen from his

35

grave in the churchyard. It was a corpse cackling away so hideously up in the scrubwood. It was a dead one coming to get him. And there—there he was, laughing aloud, right in front of him.

"Well, if it isn't Espen Kaarud!"

Did the corpse, the dead one, know him? Espen wanted to shriek, but his throat was like sand and wool. His temples pounded. He must be allowed to die a quick death—right now.

"My, my, is he running scared?"

Suddenly a blue light appeared and spread across the face of the corpse. It was blue, weary and drawn, marked by wounds and scabs.

Espen let out a loud, piercing scream.

A big, bony hand grabbed him.

"Take it easy, boy. Nothing to be afraid of."

Another voice came from the scrubwood: "Is the boy scared?"

A lantern was lit. In the glow, Espen saw two tattered, dirty fellows, with black burns on their faces, wounds on their cheeks, and scabs on their lips.

They knew him, but he did not know them. So that was how it would end: ghosts or devils would whisk him away.

"We thought we'd ask for lodging overnight at Kaarud," said the one who had grabbed Espen. "We've heard that you're staying there by yourself these days."

Slowly it dawned on Espen that they were people and not trolls. But what kind of people? Robbers?

"Ole has come home," said Espen. He thought he had better tell these outlandish brutes so they would run scared.

"You don't say? Ole has come home," repeated the other robber voice in the scrubwood. "It would be great to see him again."

"You'd better lead the way, boy," said the first robber.

37

Espen tried to calm down. These were neither ghosts nor goblins, neither wolves nor bears. They were only two robbers, and they seemed to know Ole. Maybe they were not so dangerous after all.

But he did not feel well. The fright would not let go of him. His feet stiffened. He could barely drag himself up the last few turns through the brushwood before they reached the flat ground that took them the rest of the way to Kaarud. The robber-strangers had no skis, so they plodded in the snow, huffing and puffing.

At Kaarud they were greeted by nothing but long shadows.

When Espen stepped into the cabin, the fireplace was dark, and Ole was gone.

"I don't exactly see any Ole Kaarud hanging around here," said one of the robbers. "And is it ever cold here!"

Where was his brother? Had he already returned to his army company? He had not said how long he would be staying, but Espen had thought his brother would be taking it easy for at least a couple of days. Why wasn't he there?

He could get a better look at the robbers now. They were tattered and dirty, with burnt faces and cold, shifty eyes. When they discovered that Espen was alone, they exchanged glances and looked about as if to see what they might carry away.

"There's no need to be scared," one of them said. "We have no reason to cut open your belly. If you had been a bigshot with silver dollars, we would probably have done it. Then the good Lord would have turned us into murderers, but now he has been kind enough to send us a penniless sparrow like you, and there's no reason to be hanged on account of you."

"You won't hang, Karl," said the other one. "Remember now, you'll lose your head on the block!"

Both of them roared with laughter while Espen clung to the wall.

"Do you by chance have any booze in the house?"

One of the robbers looked Espen straight in the eye. Espen shook his head—the words stuck in his throat.

The other robber, who had turned his back to him, now slowly turned around again, faced Espen, kept his eyes on him for a long time, and said:

"What's the matter with you, boy?"

Espen shook his head and tried to talk.

"You look as if you're scared to death. Do you think we are robbers?"

"Yes," Espen managed to squeak out.

The men exchanged glances again and looked a little unsure. Then they began to laugh. They were glassblowers, they said. They lived far up in the north woods and worked for Carsten Anker. It was the fire and all the glassblowing that made them look so ugly.

They were on their way to Christiania and had left a load of glassware at the estate, but then they could not find a bed down there. They had made their way up here, because they knew the people at Kaarud and Buhagen from the old days.

The next morning, the glassblowers left. Afterwards Espen wept the whole day, and once again he felt hunger gnawing at him.

Ole did not return until evening. He brought along rye, flour, and fish, for he had driven a load of scrap iron from the estate into town and had been paid for it. He was happy and cheerful, but was not able to make his younger brother laugh until late into the night.

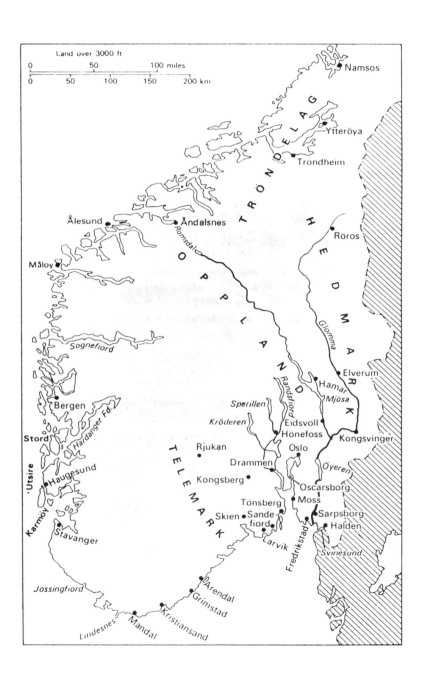

Land over 3000 ft

0   50   100 miles
0   50   100   150   200 km

Namsos

TRÖNDELAG

Ytteröya

Trondheim

HEDMARK

Röros

Ålesund

Åndalsnes

Romsdal

Elverum

OPPLAND

Måloy

Glomma

Sognefjord

Hamar
Mjösa

Randsfjord

Sperillen

Eidsvoll

Bergen

Kröderen

Hönefoss

Kongsvinger

Hardanger Fd.

Stord

Rjukan

Oslo

Drammen

Öyeren

Utsire

Haugesund

TELEMARK

Kongsberg

Oscarsborg

Tönsberg

Moss

Karmöy

Skien

Sande-
fjord

Sarpsborg

Stavanger

Larvik

Halden

Fredrikstad

Svinesund

Jössingfjord

Arendal

Grimstad

Lindesnes   Mandal

Kristiansand

III

The Parson and the Justice of the Peace

It was late in winter and the crack of dawn. Espen lay huddled in bed, sound asleep. He dreamed he heard a loon wailing, and the wailing did not stop but became a river that gushed over him. He covered his face with his hands for protection, for he did not want to drown. Waking up, he glimpsed huge shadows lying in the bed on the other side of the room. Unfamiliar clothing was hanging over the bench.

The sound came from outdoors. What was it? He padded across the ice-cold floorboards to the window. There, just outside, a hunter in a red jacket sat ramrod-straight on a dapple-white horse, blowing his trumpet. He wore a tall cap, and his pants were embroidered with golden seams.

What was this? The world looked unreal. White patches of fog hovered above the fields where the snow had begun to turn a rotten brown. Espen heard voices behind him. Someone came up and stood in the doorway next to him.

43

Little by little, it dawned on him where he was and what was happening. The rider on horseback outside was a messenger from Christian Frederik. The strange figure standing next to him was the parson from a town in the southern part of Norway. The man patting Espen's head was the justice of the peace—he also had come from the south. The day before, these two gentlemen had arrived at Kaarud, where they would be staying for some time. A few weeks before, on a church green, they had been elected to represent the people at the national assembly that was going to meet in the mansion at Eidsvoll. Over the last few days, more than a hundred people had come to the village from all over the country. They were judges and parsons, farmers and officers, merchants and commissioners.

Espen was amazed at what was happening, at all the important people coming—and two of them would be staying with him and his father! Here were no glassblowers with scabs and sores on their faces, and no cutthroats. Here were two visitors—cheerful and happy gentlemen—who had brought along flatbread, butter, dried meat, and a dram of liquor, too.

Things had gone as the captain had said that night at the estate. Prince Christian had called together a national assembly. And that thing, which had sounded so strange when he had first heard the words, now meant to him the hundred men or so who met in a big hall at the estate.

The day before, Espen had been in the ballroom while people were covering the benches with bright red cotton cloth and hanging wreaths of evergreen on the walls.

And then there were those large pictures of plump, naked women. Outside, waving in the wind, was a banner. On the banner was an enormous lion carrying an ax.

That was the Norwegian lion, he had been told.

All those men would sit there, looking at those beefy women and choose a king for Norway. They were supposed to come to an agreement about what kind of laws their country should have. And they were supposed to make Norway an independent kingdom, just as it had been in the old days, long, long ago, when the Norwegians were a great and powerful people.

And two of those who were part of it would be staying here at Kaarud. Father had been given the go-ahead to borrow a horse at the estate, so that he could drive them in a sleigh to the assembly every morning and back again every evening. That also meant that Father would come home to Espen every day. In addition, the parson and the justice of the peace would bring along food, and they were so cheerful and friendly!

But why had the rider on horseback come here so early? Was this a sign of misfortune? Had he come with bad news?

As it turned out, the rider had come with rather innocent news. It was Easter morning, a day of hope both for the people and for the country. On this day, all the representatives to the national assembly—the constitutional assembly, as they called it—were to gather in church to receive God's blessing before starting their important work.

"We need it," said the parson while they were getting the sleigh ready. "Napoleon isn't doing well, I hear. He is losing one battle after another. Soon Norway will be standing alone against all of Europe. And our generals tell us that the Norwegian army is short of powder and cannons, food and horses, bullets and guns."

Espen also went along to church. It was jam-packed with people. All the persons of importance, those who were supposed to make the laws, lined up in two rows in front of the church entrance to applaud Christian Frederik when he arrived on foot from the estate.

The prince looked more worried than the last time Espen had seen him. He did not seem to be especially cheery, perhaps because several of the representatives did not want him as king. They were the ones who would rather see Norway join Sweden, the parson had told Espen. They thought the prince wanted to become King of Norway only to tie it more firmly to Denmark. After all, he was a Danish prince, wasn't he? If he became King of Norway, the two countries would become one again, wouldn't they?

"So how do you want it?" Espen had asked the parson.

"You see, I am a red-hot democrat," chuckled the parson.

"What is a red-hot democrat?"

"It's a person who wants everyone to be allowed to say whatever he wants."

"That's one thing Jens Buhagen does," said Espen.

"What does he say then?" asked the parson.

"He says that pastors are of the devil," said Espen. But then he held his tongue, expecting the parson to become furious.

But that did not happen. "Jens Buhagen must certainly be allowed to say things much worse than that," the parson answered. "He must be allowed to say that the king is a dumbbell, that the sheriff is stupid, that the farmers should give land to the cottagers, and nobody must be able to punish him for it."

Espen stood tongue-tied and thunderstruck. Finally, he squeaked, "Do you mean it?"

Yes, he meant it. And the parson also thought that Jews and Catholics, tramps and Gypsies, and all kinds of people should be let into the country and be allowed to believe, write and say what they pleased.

"And what else?" asked Espen. He was curious to hear what this amazing parson thought.

"Otherwise I would like to have a king, but the people are supposed to govern the country. The people have received their authority from God. It is God's will for the people to govern themselves, and that's why I want us to decide here at Eidsvoll that Norway shall have a national assembly that will make laws and decisions about war and peace. Most of all, I would like to have peace always, but when the Swedes come with their cannons and swords, we won't have much choice."

"But won't Prince Christian make us join the dirty Danes again?" asked Espen.

"If Christian Frederik becomes king, he won't be able to decide that sort of thing. It is the Norwegian people who will say yes or no. And if you ask me, the answer is no."

"And if you ask me, the answer is yes," said the justice of the peace.

"The vote is one for and one against," said the parson, "so Representative Espen Kaarud has the decisive vote."

"I say no."

"Let's drink to that," laughed the justice of the peace, and he pulled out a little flask from his bag. "Come here, Sven, let's drink a toast to the first resolution passed here at Eidsvoll. Norway shall never be returned to Denmark. The motion carries with two votes in favor and one against."

On this day, over a hundred representatives would attend the first meeting of the constitutional assembly. It was Easter morning. "Let us create a nation!" was the cry. "Let us create a free country! Let us create peace and equality!"

Espen did not understand much of what happened during the church service, but he was hoping that famine would no longer lay waste the cottagers' tiny farms. He was hoping that he would not have to spend so much time alone at Kaarud. He was hoping that the wolves and the robbers would leave him alone. He was hoping that Father would soon find a wife who could also become like a mother to him.

After the church service, the trumpets sounded once again. Banners blew briskly in the wind. The justice of the peace sat down in the sleigh and declared that he had never heard a sermon more boring than the one in church today.

"Then you must have spent your time sleeping in church, my good friend," said the parson. "I can assure you that most of what is said from the pulpit these days is far worse than that."

*   *   *

This was the beginning of adventurous days for Espen. Every day, early in the morning, Father woke him up. Together with the justice of the peace and the parson, they pulled out the sleigh from the barn. Father gave the sturdy plow horse some hay and hitched him up. Then Espen wedged himself between the representatives and off they thundered down the bumpy March road. The sky was bright, a few stars swung low, the runners swished and whined in the snow, the sleigh slid along and bumped playfully over stock and stone. Now and then a rabbit would bounce across their path, occasionally they would see a moose. The parson praised the weather or told what had happened at the constitutional assembly. The justice of the peace had brought along a whole constitution in his travel bag, and he and the parson talked much about it. But they also noted that a great many constitutions had been dragged along here to Eidsvoll. People talked mostly about the one written by Christian Magnus Falsen, a judge who had become almost like a chieftain because of his suggestions.

And the parson went on: No one in the assembly could speak like Christian Magnus Falsen. Even those who disagreed with him had to rejoice. He was so enthusiastic that he carried everyone along. And they were proud of him—the pastors, the judges, the farmers—one and all.

Christian Magnus Falsen was a man of the new Norway. He did not walk around in his finery as other judges did. Oh, no, he wore everyday clothes. He was an ordinary Norwegian, a representative of the people, and he wanted to show it.

The sleigh runners were ringing as they wound their way out into the open terrain. The countryside lay before them, and farther away Espen caught a glimpse of Eidsvoll. Christian Magnus Falsen would be there and so, of course, would Espen Kaarud.

Lightning burst forth from Christian Magnus when he spoke, said the parson. Falsen reminded him of the great Norsemen of old, those who ruled the assembly—the Thing—in the olden days when the farmers were freemen and elected their own representatives to the assembly. That is how it ought to be in the new free Norway, and that is how Falsen looked at it, too. He wanted to return the power to the farmers just as King Haakon had once done. And that is why he wanted to

49

bring back solid old Norwegian words in naming this assembly of good men: they were to be called *Odelsting*, the lower house, and *Lagmannsting*, the upper house.

Wrapped in the parson's sheepskin, Espen half sat, half lay in the sleigh. He dozed, but in his mind he saw Christian Magnus Falsen stepping forth. He was tall and blond. He had gone to school in Denmark and was the smartest student in his class. Upon his return to Norway, when the war against Sweden broke out, he had quickly rallied volunteers around him. He had headed up The Bærum Corps of Volunteer Hunters, said the parson.

But he was apparently also a stubborn man, reckless and quick-tempered. There was a dark side to his life, Espen gathered, a dark side that cast shadows over his joys. His father, the well-known Enevold Falsen, had once made an unforgivable mistake. The parson did not say what it was. It was to be kept quiet. But then the same Mr. Falsen had done something even worse. He had walked from the theater in Christiania down to the docks. The next day they had found him in the wintry water.

Christian Magnus Falsen was the son of someone who had committed suicide. He could never free himself from that. Was that why he wished to become the light of the nation?

The sleigh glided the last stretch from Duck River into the estate and came to a halt. Sven Kaarud unhitched the horse. Still thinking about Christian Magnus Falsen and all the other representatives about whom the parson had spoken, Espen walked into the cowbarn and climbed up the ladder to the hayloft.

And that is where he was sitting when the parson came tiptoeing with some morsels of food for him and his father.

"This very day I have once again with God's good pleasure helped myself to another man's property," muttered the parson. He gave Espen a slab of bread, a piece of dry veal, and a few chunks of sausage.

51

The parson and the justice of the peace got their food from Elisson, the captain of the cavalry, as soon as they arrived at the estate in the morning. That was their rightful privilege, since Kaarud was located far into the woods and it was difficult to make it to the mansion early enough to eat breakfast with the others.

"Elisson has made me break the law," said the parson, "because he has tempted me to steal food for you." While saying this, he looked sternly at Espen as if to give him a guilty conscience for having done his share in luring the parson away from the straight and narrow.

But Espen ate in good conscience. And all day he walked around the buildings and thought of the wondrous things that Christian Magnus Falsen and the other strange men were doing inside the big white mansion.

What were they talking about? He could hear the sound of their voices carrying through the windows, often left open. Now and then a speaker would raise his voice, and the naked ash trees would quiver. All the way down by Duck River, one could hear a faint buzzing.

From time to time, Espen spied a rider on horseback, far off in the distance to the south of the wide-open fields. He watched each rider draw nearer, his horse steaming with sweat, his cape flowing about him. Red and flushed in the face, the officer would pull up sharply at the estate, feverishly unbutton the saddlebag and dash into the main building. The voices behind the window grew silent. Something was being announced inside.

Espen had heard that the representatives received reports from Europe about how the war was going and other big and important matters he did not understand. These riders likely carried such news.

Once in a while, some of the representatives came out and strolled about in the courtyard. They inspected the horses tied to the hitching posts by the stables, or they sauntered

52

down to Duck River. One day, no less a person than Count Herman Wedel Jarlsberg came out with Mrs. Anker. The count had trouble walking. Every step he took seemed to cause him pain.

The parson had talked much about the count, who had grown up far away, in Italy or some such place. And he had fled from his father in London and had sailed across the ocean to Denmark. Later, when the English maneuvered their battle-ships along the coast and tried to close all the harbors, he had sent food to Norway.

Was he a tramp of some kind? Espen thought that he looked dark and dangerous as he tottered along.

Mrs. Anker waved at Espen.

"Come here and say hello to a little warrior," she said to the count, and she stroked Espen on the head. Espen thought she looked grief-stricken and very sad, and wasn't that how it was?

"What is the name of this young gentleman?" asked the count.

Espen said his name, how old he was, and where he lived.

"And I understand that you have a brother who is fighting in the war?"

Yes, Espen had such a brother.

"And you would like to have him come home again, wouldn't you?"

"Yes . . . yes!"

The count cleared his throat. He leaned forward, put his hand on Espen's shoulder, tugged a bit at his jacket, shook him ever so gently, patted him under the chin, turned around and staggered into the house while Mrs. Anker tripped along behind him.

*   *   *

The days came and went. Sometimes Prince Christian Frederik and his attendants would drive into the courtyard, but he never stayed long. The parson said that the prince wanted the representatives to be able to work undisturbed. He chose not to interfere in their doings. Espen loitered about, listened and enjoyed himself.

It was often late evening or into the night before they could head home. As they left, they often heard singing and the clinking of glasses from the main building. From a little pavilion, jolly voices rose with well-wishing and shouts of "Cheers!" Sitting in the sleigh, they could also hear the hurrahs, the singing, the laughter, and the band playing. And the many tinkling sounds would blend with the meowing runners of the sleigh. On the other side of the fields in the woodland, a bonfire flared in the dark: a signal from a camp, soldiers on watch.

The March shadows grew darker as they came closer to the forest, which was no longer as frightening as it had been earlier in the winter—now it was blue and secretive. The clinking from the mansion sounded even more cheerful here at the edge of the forest. Espen simply could not understand how anybody in there could be at odds or in disagreement. Weren't they all jumping for joy?

The way he understood it, two large groups were struggling for power. In the one group, Christian Magnus Falsen was the chieftain. This group rallied around Christian Frederik and wanted Carl Johan and the Swedes to go jump in the lake.

In the other group, Count Hermann Wedel Jarlsberg—no less—was the chieftain. Those who rallied around him also wanted to govern the country from Eidsvoll, and they wanted to make a deal with Carl Johan and the Swedes. They wanted the constitutional assembly not only to give Norway a constitution, but also to take over the helm after completing that work.

Well, well, thought Espen, that last part wasn't worth fighting about. But he understood the part about the Swedes. He had not forgotten what Ole had said: Norway could just as well be subject to Sweden as long as Victoria got enough green grass.

"We are all hoping for a better life," said the justice of the peace.

"Amen," replied the parson, and they drove into the forest, where the parson and the justice of the peace stepped out of the sleigh and walked alongside it. Only Espen was seated in the sleigh, for he had dozed off and was still fast asleep when they glided into the March-blue clearing, with the wind howling under the open starry sky, and came to a halt before the low, rundown buildings at Kaarud.

Sven carried his son inside.

"We have to set our hopes on boys like him," said the parson.

"It will be a hundred years before cottagers and servants have a part in making decisions and in electing representatives to the national assembly," said the justice of the peace. "That is, if it ever happens."

"I thought you wanted none of such ideas," answered the parson. "I thought I was the only genuine democrat."

"On a night in March such as this, it can happen to anyone," smiled the justice of the peace.

"The age of miracles is here," laughed the parson, "and spring is yet to come."

IV

A Young Nation

The days ran their course in April and early May. Snow and then sun, rain and then wind. The white fields turned a pale brown along the edges. Soon black patches began to appear and grow in size, and the roads took on the color of dirt. It was no longer possible to drive the sleigh. Sven had received the go-ahead from the estate owner's right-hand man to use a carriage because Carsten Anker had long since left for London to speak for Norway. He was trying to make the English understand that the Norwegians did not want to give in to Sweden. They would rather fight to the last man, burn their own houses and huts, and hang every Norwegian who gave up instead of fighting.

Carsten Anker did not say this in so many words, but in the constitutional assembly, noted the parson, there were many furious warriors who had made the prince's motto their own: "Death or freedom is our watchword."

59

"I think the Swedes are scared of us," said the parson to Espen one evening in May. "You know, those mighty Swedish kings have tried to conquer Norway again and again. Erik XIV and Charles XII were both warrior-kings and defeated the Russians and the Danes, but the Swedish bullies have never quite pulled it off with the Norwegians. They do well on the Russian steppes and down on the flats of Scania, but when a Swede turns up in a Norwegian valley, he is not the bigshot he is in Europe.

"Even so, we shouldn't fight this time," said the parson. "People are starving to death all over the country. People are swelling up from hunger. They are perishing for lack of fish, meat, and grain. A country that is so poverty-stricken cannot carry on a war. What a sacrifice that would take!"

Espen gathered that in most respects the parson and the justice of the peace were well pleased with what had been decided at the national assembly.

"We shall no longer have counts, barons, knights, and dukes in this country," said the justice of the peace. "No one will have a special advantage over anyone else. And that also applies to owners of sawmills, fisheries, and ironworks. Besides, everyone must serve as a soldier."

"Everyone has the duty and the right to defend the fatherland," said the parson. "What do you think of that, Espen?"

Espen thought that sounded fair and square.

"In our village, Ole, Nils, and other cottagers' sons are the ones who have to serve as soldiers," he said. "The Swedes will feel the heat when those fellows begin to fight. And when all those other fellows become soldiers, my, my, poor Swedes!"

"The new national assembly will be named the Big Thing—the Storting," said the justice of the peace one day. "It is an odd name, almost an un-thing, a nuisance, I think, even if the name does come from the old Norway when we had a 'Thing,' that is, a public assembly in every region of our country."

"At any rate, it is no small thing," answered the parson.

In listening to the two representatives, Espen had gathered that the constitutional assembly was drawing to a close. He noticed that, lately, they had almost seemed to be under a spell. It was as if the *hulder* or the trolls had given them a magic potion and made them forget the world from which they came. The big, white building at the estate was the enchanted castle itself. It bewitched those who entered it and transformed them.

Suddenly the weather also turned bewitched. The cold loosened its grip, and warmth flowed through the countryside. The buds burst forth, the green birches sailed up the slopes, and the white anemones floated in sheets through the undergrowth.

At the estate, judges, commissioners, pastors, and officers suddenly showed up in uniform. On May 16 the elected representatives signed the constitution.

When Sven drove them to the estate the next day, the parson said, "Yesterday we signed the constitution. Today we will elect a king."

"Today Norway will become an independent country, today is a festive day. We will never forget May 17," exclaimed the justice of the peace.

When the men had been delivered inside, Espen could still hear them very clearly. The windows were open. The larks were singing at a feverish pitch. Inside the building, strong voices shouted hurrah, hurrah, hurrah. And when the whole assembly came out into the courtyard a little later, many of them were weeping.

"Everyone voted for Christian Frederik," cried the parson. "Everyone agrees now and will remain faithful until the Dovre Mountains fall! Norway has now become one of the nations of Europe, the youngest nation anywhere, Espen, just an infant, a newborn babe among nations!"

Later in the evening, upon their return to Kaarud, they heard the cuckoo calling. The grass was as soft as down, the birches nodded in the spring night, mist rose from the ground. Espen had fallen asleep in the carriage but woke up when—bumpitty-thud—they crossed the creek and headed down the homestretch. He felt joy rippling through his body, for now summer would be here, and the meadows would sprout with sorrel and timothy grass.

"I wish I could turn this country into poetry," said the parson. "But I know it can't be done. Words fail me."

*   *   *

The carriage wheels rattled across rocks and stones. No one said anything. If the parson could not find the words, who could?

Espen heard the parson's voice as if he were speaking from under a carpet of moss. "We keep our country closed to Jews and Jesuits. We also say no to monks who might wish to move north to this country. We fear what we have no reason to fear, then we embrace what we ought to avoid."

"And what is that?" asked the justice of the peace.

"It is injustice, my good friend," answered the parson. "We hold on to that, don't we? We have taken it with us, even into our young nation."

In the time that followed, Espen roamed the woods every day. The parson and the justice of the peace had left. The perch and the char were feeding in ponds and lakes. He whittled himself a rod and fished in the lakes and the streams. He jumped from stone to stone in the rivers, followed the brooks up the mountainsides, and climbed the rocky slopes. At Black Pond he built himself a hunter's shelter, and far inside Sevenboy Bog he kept watch at night, waiting for grouse.

One day, the scent of the bird cherry stung his nostrils. It came so sharply that he almost lost his breath, and he knew once again that he was quite alone in the woods. His mother's eyes looked upon him from a hillside covered in green. He thought that life lay ahead of him, but there also had to be someone who cared about him—otherwise life would not be worth living, no matter how often spring returned.

Where was Espen's father? He was down by the estate, of course, but where was he otherwise in this world? Espen sensed that he was about to disappear somewhere. He was on a journey to a country called old age, and that was far away. Espen could not reach it. Some day he might also go on a journey to old age, but by then his father would have left it.

Each one has his own forest, his own pond, his own cherry blossoms. Each one reaches them alone, sees them alone, smells them alone. Each person has his joys by himself, his sorrows by himself.

But this was not clear to Espen. He lived somewhere between tears and happiness.

The mountain ash bloomed. The warm weather continued, and the forest smelled like dried grain. Father had plowed the fields at Kaarud. They were sprouting and growing well. Perhaps there would be a bumper crop this year; perhaps there would be peace and plenty, Father had said one evening when he returned to the farm.

But one day in July, a rumor ran through the village: Peace was breaking up. War was on the way. England was against the new nation. Napoleon had been defeated for good and had been shipped to an island out in the ocean. Russia and Austria demanded that the Norwegians give themselves up to the Swedes.

War was knocking at the door. People shrugged their shoulders and did not want to believe it.

"It is nothing but tricks and lies," said Jens Buhagen. "The king will take care of us, and he has God on his side."

V

The King Who Wept

At the beginning of August, Ole came home. Espen was milking Victoria down in the outpasture when Ole arrived. First his hair came into view, then his face, then his smile—a faint and forlorn smile. Espen could see right away that something was wrong. When he ran through the grass toward his brother, the bees and the mosquitoes, the houseflies, and the horseflies told him that something was not right. They were humming loudly.

And there stood his brother, as tattered and dirty as the time before, with white tape around his thigh and his arm in a sling. Ole brought big news.

"Well, the war is here," he barely managed to say. "But here am I, and I am alive."

He raised his voice as if wanting to ask if he was in fact alive and standing in the pasture right there and then. Amazed and confused, he looked at his brother Espen and at Victoria as if he did not quite believe what he was seeing.

"What is it with you? What has happened to you?" Espen had a hard time speaking.

Ole lifted his hand.

"Two shots," he said, "one in the arm and one in the thigh. The army surgeon cut out the bullets. The war is on now, Espen."

Ole looked at his brother for a long time. He smiled so strangely, and, once again, Espen heard the flies and the grasshoppers. Ole sat down on the grass.

"There were five hundred of us at the embankments at Veden," said Ole. "That's in Tistedal, down by Halden. On the first of August, the Swedes made their move."

And Ole told his story. The Swedish battalion had attacked at the ford by the Tista River. Their cannons had appeared on the shores of the river and on the stony ridges beyond. The Swedes had opened heavy fire, stormed through the brush and out into the water, toward the tiny bridge that spanned the river.

Ole had been sitting in the camp, between the carts and the tents, when the Swedes attacked. The bullets whistled past, smashed one of the luggage carts, crushed a soldier's leg, blasted the head off another. Suddenly the soldiers roared, shouted, screamed, ran back and forth, grabbed their guns and stormed down to the embankment.

They had been waiting for the Swedes for several days, and they remembered quite clearly what the brigadier had said: Don't shoot without hitting the target and not until the enemy is close to you. Run, attack and use your bayonet. Take three enemies with you into the next life.

Ole remembered this, even if he had an iron claw squeezing his heart. He remembered it even when his friend Nils was knocked off his feet at the edge of the river and lay there on the rocky shoreline, shouting. He shouted for his mother and doubled up.

By then, the first Swede had crossed the river. Ole saw him at once. Behind him, more blue soldiers stormed ahead with raised bayonets. Right and left, Ole saw his buddies rushing to the scene in their gray, worn uniforms. They were pulling an old luggage cart. Some of them leaned against the sideboards, put their flintlocks on the ironclad wheel for support, aimed, and waited.

Ole scampered up to the Swede, looked him quickly in the eye and realized that he was standing face-to-face with another cottager's son. Someone who came from the backwoods just as he did. Who was scared spitless just as he was. Who may not have been as poor, as starved, as furious, but someone to talk with rather than to kill.

But there was only one thing to do. They charged at each other. The Swede lost his footing on the slippery rocks by the river, and that did it. Ole thrust the bayonet straight into his belly.

By then a new Swede had appeared with raised bayonet. The Swede was just about to nail Ole when his face froze. Nils Buhagen had fired his flintlock. Then a cannon, a Swedish three-pounder, belched from the brushwood on the other side. Nils stretched out his arms and floated down the river.

"I couldn't believe it," said Ole. "Nils Buhagen floating downstream. It couldn't be true. It had to be a lie."

Ole had scrambled after his friend and hauled him ashore. But now the Swedes came in full force, men on foot and on horseback buzzed across the river. The Norwegians had to pull back behind the embankment. A couple of fellows from Lærdal managed to drag Ole with them.

Five hundred Norwegians were encamped there. There must have been thousands of Swedes. They stormed five times.

"We drove them back every time," said Ole. "We were going to fight to the last man. That's how stark, raving mad we were. We were going to die for Christian Frederik and the fatherland and all that. We shouted hurrah and died, or we roared with pain, lying there blinded by shots, without sense, without hope.

"The infantry surgeon ran about and cut out cannon splinters and bullets from arms, legs, and bellies. He was confused or drunk or both."

When the Swedes attacked the embankment for the third time, Ole felt a stinging pain in his thigh. Afterwards the surgeon flipped out the bullet. It sat loose on the outside of a bone. The gunshot wound in his arm was only a scratch, but on the way home the wound had become infected.

"We finally had to pull back. The commander gave the orders. We dragged ourselves northward to Smaalenene, where we met other battalions that had also withdrawn. The Swedes moved forward with bunches of battalions and with cannons everywhere, and we pulled back. We would rather have fought to the last man, Espen. The lieutenants, the captains, the colonels wanted it, and the soldiers, too. We were all wild enough to do it, and we knew that our Norwegian wildness is what the Swedes fear the most."

"Yah?"

Espen gasped and gushed with curiosity. He turned now warm, now cold, filled with eagerness and horror.

"But the generals didn't want it anymore. People say that the king didn't want it either. At any rate, he wept when he saw us."

"He wept?"

"Yes, he wept when he saw the cart with the wounded. I don't know who is smarter, those of us who wanted to fight or the king who wept."

"A king is not supposed to weep, is he, Ole?"

"No, maybe not, not a Norwegian king anyway."

* * *

But what will become of Norway?

Many wondered about that. There were rumors that the king was thinking about surrendering, and that Carl Johan wanted to conquer the country. Rumor also had it that people resented the generals' not daring to go after the Swedes. The soldiers wanted to hang the generals and start the fighting again, it was said.

What will become of Norway?

Down at Buhagen, the women wept, and Jens Buhagen sat stone-faced and stared off into space. Nils had been laid out and was soon to be buried. It was like a strange sign to see the village suddenly flooded in sunshine. The grain turned yellow, the dust whipped along the roads, the narrow hayfields shone brown and dry.

What will become of Norway?

Espen now had his brother Ole back at Kaarud again. Even with Ole's wounds, the two of them dug up plenty of fat, dirty worms from the manure pile behind the cowbarn and hiked up to Black Pond with their fishing rods. The trout began to bite, and they lingered into the night, while the daddy longlegs flitted about and the bats fluttered against the August sky.

Both of them had a feeling that other brothers had done this before them. Brothers had cleared patches of land for hayfields far into the woods, had fished in the lakes and the ponds, set traps for rabbits and grouse, walked the invisible pathways into the deep forest.

But what would become of Ole?

The thought struck Espen with a wave of worry. His brother had become so pale and weak. The wound on his arm ached and throbbed. He had taken a trip down to the estate, and an infantry surgeon from Minnesund had cleaned the wound and put on a new dressing.

But a few days later, the thigh also swelled up. Angry lines ran up toward Ole's hips. He gave his brother a faint smile, stroked him on the head, and looked out over the village countryside toward the outer reaches of the forest where land rose into sky.

"You mustn't get sick, Ole!"

It came as a loud cry.

Ole tugged him by the hair.

"I'm doing my best, Espen."

He had again dragged himself down to the infantry surgeon, but had returned sad-faced and downcast. He was silent and weary.

Espen watched him with anxious eyes, and every morning he searched his brother's face for signs of health. Now and then it seemed as if his brother perked up, and sometimes Ole told stories from the military camp by Lake Øyeren, where he had been on patrol as late as mid-July. But then his head would soon droop again, and he had to lie down on the bunk.

One day at the break of dawn, Espen was awakened by his brother's heavy groaning. Red blotches moved in flashes across his brother's cheeks and forehead. Espen tiptoed outside and dashed down to the estate. He found his father in the stables and threw himself, crying, into his arms:

"You must get a doctor, Father. Ole is sick. He has to be taken to the camp hospital!"

Father freed himself.

"Espen, it's no use with Ole."

"Have you talked with the surgeon?"

"No, but I can tell from the way Ole is."

"You must get help, Father!"

"It's no use, Espen."

The son's voice faded to a whisper. He felt heavy and dead. On the way home, he lay by the roadside and sobbed. He did not reach Kaarud until midday. By then he had cried himself dry and felt as if he had been beaten to a pulp.

Ole was sitting in the August sun by the south wall. He was pale and sweaty. He had cut open his gray uniform to make room for the arm and the thigh. They had swelled up immensely.

Upon seeing Espen, he managed to force a smile.

"Our fishing days are over now," Ole said.

Espen could not see his brother for his tears.

"Can you imagine a cottager bum with one arm and one leg?" asked Ole. "What kind of life would that have been in our village? Do you think I want to be a cripple and ruin my brother's life?"

"Don't say that," wept Espen.

"But that's what the infantry surgeon said. 'I'll have to remove your leg and your arm, good man.' That's what he

73

said. 'Then maybe we'll be able to save your life. . . . ' But I wouldn't be able to take that. You understand, don't you, Espen? I want us to be able to remember a good life together, you and me, Espen. You're going to remember me as Ole the soldier, not as Ole the cripple."

Espen could not understand. He lay on the ground and cried. When he had run out of tears, he fell asleep, and when he woke up Ole had perked up a bit. He managed to drag himself down to the millstream where the brothers would catch minnows. Later in the evening, Father arrived. He brought a bottle of hard liquor from Elisson, the captain of the cavalry, who was visiting the estate and had heard that Ole was in a bad way. Espen now thought that Ole would get well again. And Father seemed to be so young and strong that night, just as if he had unloaded a big burden.

In the night, Espen dreamed that big black birds flew over Kaarud. They wailed and swooped down toward the buildings as if they wanted to take something away with them. Their wings blocked out the sun and left a chill.

What was that?

Espen sat up in bed. Ole was shouting crazily. Espen could not understand what he was saying. The words were jumbled. Espen could barely make out his own name, that was all he could understand. Ole was drenched with sweat and flailed about with his arms.

"Ole," exclaimed Espen, and rushed over to shake him. But his brother wailed and was out of his senses. He struggled with his arms, whimpered, and let out long ooh-ing sounds, but he did not come to.

Father stepped up to Espen.

"Run down to Buhagen and get Ingrid," said Father. Espen scrambled downhill. The air had taken on a breath of coolness.

Ingrid promptly joined him, heading uphill. She took his hand. He was thinking that what was happening right now was

not happening. He was dreaming, or he did not exist.

"Let's hope it will go fast with Ole," said Ingrid.

That wish was fulfilled. The next day, late in the afternoon, she came out to Espen, who was taking a nap by the south wall. She stroked his hair, patted him gently on the cheek, washed away the grimy streaks on his face with cold water, and said that Ole was now out of his misery.

Espen knew it was a lie. Ole could not be gone. The day before they had been fishing together in the creek. He had been standing out there on the hill with a smile on his face. He had not looked that healthy in a long time.

The world had come to a standstill. He felt no sorrow, no pain. He knew that his brother was alive and Ingrid had made a big mistake. His brother had returned to his combat unit, where he was needed. There was going to be another fight with the Swedes.

Many days passed before he realized that Ingrid had spoken the truth. He saw Ole lying motionless in bed; he saw him placed in the grave; he heard the pastor offer thanks to the brave, fallen soldier. But all this was also a lie. Ole was up in the woods. He would much rather be a Swede or a trapper or an outlaw.

In the evenings, Espen cried. There were times when he pounded his hands bloody against the wall and banged his head against the ground.

Ole was not here anymore. Slowly Espen began to understand what had happened. He had lost the most beloved person, his only friend, in this life.

VI

The Prince Journeys Back

The war was over. Espen barely listened to the rumors running wild through the countryside. The Norwegians had withdrawn their troops. The Swedes no longer advanced. The Storting, the national assembly, had come together again. The Norwegians were trying to reach an agreement with the Swedes.

"Are we going to unite with Sweden after all?" some asked.

Others asked, "Can Norway become a free country, an independent country, united with Sweden—in a union, as they call it?"

Carl Johan waited in Halden, his troops on Norwegian soil. But the national assembly was in session. The president of the assembly, Wilhelm Friman Koren Christie, insisted that Norway must keep its independence. People said that he frightened the Swedes because he was so fearless. He would rather wage another war than have the country lose its constitution, its elected assembly, its courts, and its army.

But Christian Frederik was ready to give up the Norwegian throne, people said. He did not dare take up the battle against Carl Johan. He had said himself that he could best serve the people by withdrawing and making peace.

"He will not give up the throne," said Christie. "The constitutional assembly elected him king. Only a new assembly can release him from his sacred duty. However, if it is the wish of this assembly to . . ."

"We must reach a solution to this matter," said Carl Johan. "We are becoming impatient. How will you Norwegians stand up against us if your unreasonable demands cannot be met?"

"With desperation, gentlemen," said Christie to the Swedish representatives. "We will fight to the last man."

Those Norwegians were crazier than bedbugs. Those Norbugs, as the Swedes said.

But wasn't peace the best thing? Hadn't the Norwegians gone hungry long enough during these many years of war? Hadn't they starved to death? Hadn't they died from sickness and shortages of food?

The misery and the poverty were horrible. Beggars were seen everywhere; so were orphans, homeless, cripples, corpses.

"Desperation, gentlemen," exclaimed Christie, who with his firm stand put the fear of God into the Swedes.

But shouldn't brothers be able to live together in peace?

*   *   *

The grain fields were turning yellow, the leaves on the

80

The grain fields were turning yellow, the leaves on the trees beginning to fade.

"Desperation," declared Christie to Sweden's chief representative, General Björnstjärna.

"You may have some luck this fall if you attack right away. Perhaps you will conquer the country as far north as Eidsvoll. But then the Norwegian winter will creep up on you. Carl Johan is from the warm shores of Pau, at the southern tip of France. Does he realize what will happen when his victorious Swedish army is attacked by the stinging cold? Does he realize what will happen in the narrow Norwegian valleys when, like bobcats, the Norwegians pounce upon the Swedes? Our country is made for winter wars, for ambushes and invisible companies of skiers dashing across the snow at the speed of lightning."

"The Norwegians had better obey the Swedish king and submit to Swedish superiority," insisted General Björnstjärna.

"We demand independence," Christie flashed back. "If we do not get it, we will respond with desperation. We demand that in Norway only Norwegians be judges, magistrates, officers, and pastors. In other words, no Swedes. We demand further that the Norwegian national assembly have greater power than the king, especially since the king is now going to be Swedish."

In every township throughout the country, people were talking about what was happening—at every village inn, at every marketplace.

The October wind blew across the land. Leaves were falling, sweeping across the fields, whirling into the sea, flying across the docks. A boat cloaked itself in the night. Pulleys squeaked, booms creaked. It was a two-masted ship sailing past Nesodden by Christiania.

Christian Frederik was leaving the country. Norway's first elected king was departing. The table had been cleared for

Carl Johan. Christian Frederik boarded the ship *Alart* out in the fjord.

The sea rose and fell in black and white. The rain whipped across reefs and shores. Stormy winds approached from the North Sea and whirled their way up the fjord.

Christian Frederik was not leaving the country after all? His ship lay at anchor outside Command Island by Stavern. Word sped across the nation and reached Carl Johan. The Swedish crown prince was furious.

"Desperation, sir," the prince was told. "The national assembly has not yet said yes to Christian Frederik's resignation. The Norwegian assembly has not yet elected a new king."

Once again Espen was by himself at Kaarud. Rain whipped up the fields. Brooks overflowed. He rarely walked in the woods these days. He preferred to stay close to home.

dashed into Kaarud. Espen must come right away. It was urgent.

Espen wondered why his father had not come to get him. But at the estate, Father had made a rig ready and was impatiently pacing back and forth in the courtyard. Two horses had been hitched up. A trunk had been loaded onto the carriage. Two officers talked with Father.

"You are going with me, Espen," Father said hurriedly.

"What is it? Where are we going?"

"You are a courier, my boy," said one of the officers. "You are a messenger."

Espen looked from the officer's face to his father's. "Where are we going?"

"We are leaving now," said Father. He lifted the boy up onto the carriage, jumped into the driver's seat, grabbed the reins and cracked the whip. The rain poured down upon them. The wheels chattered, the rig thumped ahead.

*   *   *

"What are we going to do with that trunk?" asked Espen, after they had driven a couple of miles.

"It's for King Christian," answered his father.

Espen did not seem the least bit surprised that they were supposed to bring a trunk to King Christian.

"And what is King Christian going to do with it?"

"That's a secret," answered the father, and gave him a sidelong look. "I don't even know."

"What's in the trunk?"

The father did not know that either. "He is supposed to get it before he leaves the country. He's waiting for this trunk. He won't depart until he receives it."

Espen did not ask any more.

"People say he has become a bit strange," said the father.

"Who?"

"They say that King Christian has gone mad."

"What is he going to do with the trunk?"

The father fell silent.

"Somebody on horseback is following us," said Espen.

"Two cavalry men," answered the father. "They are supposed to accompany us the whole way."

"Who is sending the trunk?"

"The king's best friend, Carsten Anker, prepared it, and Mrs. Anker asked me to bring a greeting from her."

"But why are the two soldiers following us?"

"There are many spies on the roads. Carl Johan has his boys round about. Many are siding with the Swedes these days."

"Are they after the trunk?"

"Maybe. They sneak around everywhere."

"They shouldn't have taken Ole away from us, Father."

Sven Kaarud seemed taken aback, as if he had not expected this. The words stung him, and he visibly wrestled with his thoughts before answering.

"God's ways are unknowable, my son," he said softly. "His ways often lead through the roughest rapids."

"Our Lord cannot look upon us with kindness when he behaves that way."

"You mustn't say that. God wanted it that way, and we don't know why. First he took Mother, then Ole. He punishes us for our sins, and he determines our continued pilgrimage on this earth. We need to bow our heads humbly."

"He is a devil, that's what he is," charged Espen.

"Hush, boy, somebody may hear you. Perhaps Carl Johan's spies are listening in the bushes right there!" Father pointed to a clump of alder ahead on the side of the road.

"There?" Espen also pointed.

"Yes, right there. They are after the trunk. It could hold some secrets of war or perhaps gold."

Espen did not answer. He cast a glance far out toward the horizon as if his thoughts were in another world.

They drove on. In the evening, they arrived at Bragernes. They stopped in front of an inn and carried the trunk upstairs to a room that had been reserved for them. The soldiers checked in at the same inn.

They went to bed early, feeling beaten and tired after a long day's ride over bumpy roads. The wind lulled them to sleep as it whistled around the gables. Having come closer to the coast, they noticed the first signs of the storm that had raged there for the last week.

In the middle of the night, Espen woke up. It was pitch dark. He thought he heard a scratching sound as if something were being dragged across the floor.

"Father!" he shouted. "Somebody is in the room!"

There was a thump. Father bounced out of bed and scrambled headlong across the floor in the direction of the trunk.

"Help!" shouted Espen. He heard muffled blows and shouts and realized that people were rolling around, striking at one another. The sound of running boots could be heard on the staircase. Someone yanked at the door, but it was locked. Then a heavy body threw itself with a bang against the door.

"They are running off with King Christian's trunk," shouted Father.

Just then, a gust of wind burst into the room. The curtains flapped to one side. Espen caught a glimpse of the trunk in the open window where a dark figure was about to tip it out.

"They are running off with King Christian's trunk!" screamed Espen once again in a shrill voice, just as the trunk was tipped out of the window with the dark figure following it. Then the door sprang open. The two soldiers rushed in, holding a kicking body high in the air. It was none other than the innkeeper who had received them the day before.

Now angry shouts could be heard from below. Espen and the soldiers ran to the window and saw the trunk lying half smashed on the street, with open lid and splintered boards. Next to it, a few sailors were holding a kicking fellow.

"Here we have the crook," said one of them, looking up at Espen and the soldiers in the window.

"He's a Swedish spy," shouted one of the soldiers. "Hold on to him until we come down."

"Hang the Swedish spy!" boomed a voice from the tavern, where some dock workers were still drinking it up.

The soldiers, Father, and Espen stomped down the stairs. Out in the street, Espen could barely make out dark bodies, waving arms, and faint yellow candlelight coming from some windows.

"Hang the Swedish spy!" some people shouted again, as large black figures staggered toward them. One of them held a flickering, sleepy oil lamp in his hand.

A couple of loose trunk boards dangled in the wind. The light danced across the dirt road, across shuffling feet, across puddles, down into the trunk.

Espen pushed his way between the dark bodies. What was in the trunk? Just what were they supposed to bring to Christian Frederik? What were the thieves after?

The glow from the lamp floated closer to the trunk, hesitated a bit, and then fell upon the contents.

First a red uniform jacket came into view, then some books, then a few documents, a little silver box, and a couple of pistols. No royal crown, no ghosts were hidden in the trunk, not a single thing that could work a change in the dark street, the dark figures, or the painful knot in the pit of Espen's stomach.

The soldiers and the sailors led the innkeeper and the thief, name unknown, over to the town jail. When they returned, it was quiet in both the tavern and the inn. Espen lay awake, waiting for his father.

"No one is shouting hurrah anymore," he said. "No one shouts hurrah for King Christian. No one shouts 'Long live the king!'"

"He is not a king anymore," said Father, who seemed to have a hard time removing himself from where he stood because he said that Espen's eyes shone so strangely in the dark. Once again they heard the storm tearing at the low wooden houses in Bragernes, and suddenly everything seemed so far off—Eidsvoll, Kaarud, and all the worries at home.

On the evening of that same day, they reached Stavern. Once again it was raining cats and dogs. They felt beaten to a pulp after their trip through Vestfold. In Stavern, the commander at the fortress sent a boat out to the ship *Alart* to tell Christian Frederik that an old peasant and his son had come with a trunk from Carsten Anker or some such person.

Prince Christian Frederik—he called himself prince now—let them know that the peasant and his son were to be rowed out to the *Alart* and brought on board.

"Now, my friend," he said to Sven. "What brings you to the outcast Prince Christian? Are you a messenger from Ariel, the airy spirit, bringing news that the weather will soon be good for sailing to Denmark?"

Sven stood dumbfounded at this greeting. But Espen responded, "We have come with a trunk. It's from Eidsvoll."

"My little lad," said the prince. "Haven't I seen you before?"

Espen told him where they had last met.

"Those were happy days," said the prince.

"They were," said Espen, and looked down.

The prince asked him if he too had suffered a loss.

"It's my brother," said Espen. "He is gone on a journey, far out in the universe."

"He is dead," said his father, who stood in the background. "He was mortally wounded at Veden."

The prince fell silent. Outside, the wind tore wildly. The white, frothy surf surged across the gray rocks, gurgled, sputtered, and sprayed the deck.

"God's hand is merciless, and no one knows where his sword strikes," said Christian. "My grief is small, and my ability to grieve is even smaller. Tomorrow we sail for Denmark. Farewell, gentlemen."

He shook hands with both of them. Father and son were rowed ashore. On their way back, while passing through Christiania, they learned that the national assembly had just elected Swedish Carl XIII Johan King of Norway. Nobody shouted hurrah.

*　　*　　*

"I can't take care of Kaarud any longer," said Father to the land manager at the estate.

"We'll have to lease the farm to somebody else," said the manager.

Espen said nothing.

"Do we have to move from Kaarud now?" he asked Father.

"If Ole had been alive, we would probably have been able to live here, but as for the two of us . . ."

Sven Kaarud did not complete his answer.

The new age did not belong to him. He had lost. Whether Norway had won or lost was no longer of interest to Sven Kaarud. He wanted to leave Kaarud and go to work full time at the Eidsvoll Estate, and he had to take Espen with him. He knew that Espen would suffer. But Carsten Anker had promised to have the private tutor at the estate give Espen some extra lessons. At the estate, he would also meet other children looked after by the tutor, children to whom the new age belonged.

Rumor had it that Sven Kaarud was not the only one who had lost. Things had also gone bad for Carsten Anker, who had borrowed money all over the world and could not pay it back. The glassworks were no longer profitable. Misery and poverty were knocking at the glassblowers' door, and Carsten Anker was nearly bankrupt.

*   *   *

One day in December, Espen and his father moved from Kaarud. Enormous amounts of snow had fallen, and the chill had set in. Sven had borrowed a sled and was loading their tools and trunks. There was not much to bring along.

Standing in the small farmyard, Espen looked out over the forestland. Black Pond lay far inland, and Sevenboy Bog and the wild woods even farther. In days gone by, outlaws had

90

roamed there. He felt a fist in his heart. Where it had once been soft and tender, it was now hard and tense.

He had lived and experienced those days at the Eidsvoll Estate near Duck River. People in the village talked about the work of freedom, and, when recalling what had happened during those weeks in spring, they made it sound like a beautiful song. But Espen knew that this melody was not his, not yet anyway. Perhaps someday in the future, he could hum that tune of freedom. Perhaps he carried within him a longing for another life, a better life, than the one he had endured as a cottager's son.

Espen walked slowly behind the sled that carried the last few meager possessions away from Kaarud. He looked out over the old fields, the stone fences, and the old trails that came into view so clearly when the frost set in and told the story of times past, how the people who went before made tracks in the landscape that others followed.

Espen walked heavyheartedly, leaving deep footprints in the snow. The darkness swallowed him slowly. Finally, only the sled runners sang from a new age.

Afterword

In this book about Espen, Karsten Alnæs presents us with a crucial chapter and dimension in the life of the Norwegian people. Important national events taking place in 1814 are seen through the eyes of the common people. Two levels of lived reality come into play: Happenings on a large, political scale are experienced on a small, personal scale. This perspective leads to a new understanding of what stirred the Norwegian people at depth. The book's setting also sheds considerable light on the sparse conditions under which those people lived.

Books on the genesis of the Norwegian constitution ordinarily present us with a small group of personalities who possessed the knowledge to get the job done. In fact, only a small elite, a very limited circle, knew anything about polity, forms of government, and institutions—apart from the fact that there was a royal tradition deeply rooted in the populace. This tradition received a democratic imprint in the constitution that saw the light of day on May 17, 1814. Since that time, both the constitution and the king have become unifying symbols. Both are viewed as guaranteeing justice and the rule of law.

The constitution of 1814 makes no passionate declarations about freedom, equality, or brotherhood. In its Norwegian form, the constitution was a realistic manifestation of equality and brotherhood—imperfect, to be sure, but more truthful than in other European countries, where the royal court and the nobility made up a nation of their own. Although the persons giving shape to the constitution of 1814 were an elite group, the work at Eidsvoll became the work of *the people*. With time, it has become the property of the *whole* people.

In a unique way, the story about Espen, his forefathers and descendants, places the events of 1814 in a rightful historical context. It may seem paradoxical that the Norwegian Monarchy, more than anything else, embodies a unity and a solidarity that no social, political or economic disagreements have managed to disrupt. The king has become an independent cohesive force for the nation, a force that stands above party politics. The Norwegian people do not want a "strong, uncontested" leader. Our ideals are of a different kind. We wanted and we received a government of the people, a church of the people, and a king of the people. What has happened since 1814 has been a beneficial gift to Espen's descendants.

In this book, Karsten Alnæs has wisely and creatively allowed two sides of the same story to illuminate each other. *The Boy from Duck River* constitutes captivating literature of the highest quality and public enlightenment of the best kind.

Jo Benkow
President Ret.
The Parliament of Norway